# HEATH'S HOMECOMING

MERRY FARMER

# HEATH'S HOMECOMING

Copyright ©2018 by Merry Farmer

This ebook is licensed for your personal enjoyment only. This ebook may not be re-sold or given away to other people. If you would like to share this book with another person, please purchase an additional copy for each recipient. If you're reading this book and did not purchase it, or it was not purchased for your use only, then please return to your digital retailer and purchase your own copy. Thank you for respecting the hard work of this author.

This book is a work of fiction. Names, characters, places, and incidents are products of the author's imagination or are used fictitiously. Any resemblance to actual events or locales or persons, living or dead, is entirely coincidental.

Cover design by

ASIN: B079YTQ6WL

Paperback ISBN: 9781980459583

Click here for a complete list of other works by Merry Farmer.

If you'd like to be the first to learn about when the next books in the series come out and more, please sign up for my newsletter here: http://eepurl.com/RQ-KX

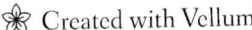 Created with Vellum

# BE SURE TO READ ALL SIX BOOKS IN THE LANGLEY LEGACY SERIES

*"Beare and Forebeare"* (*be patient and endure*)

Meet the Langley's who've traveled from their homeland of Ireland with only what they could carry. Along with the meager possessions brought from their homeland of Ireland, were a piece of lace and a silver pocket watch with the family motto "Beare and Forebearc" inscribed inside.

When the Langley's settled in New Dawn Springs, Oregon, little did they suspect the land would be a legacy to those who would come after them and that the land would be owned by the family for generations to come.

Follow the Langley's rich family history through the years as told through the wonderful storytelling voices of these six bestselling authors.

1850 - FINN'S FORTUNE, by Kathleen Ball
1875 - PATRICK'S PROPOSAL, by Hildie McQueen
1899 - DONOVAN'S DECEIT, by Kathy Shaw
1933 - AIDAN'S ARRANGEMENT, by Peggy McKenzie
1968 - HEATH'S HOMECOMING, by Merry Farmer
Present Day - COLLIN'S CHALLENGE, by Sylvia McDaniel

# 1

NEW DAWN SPRINGS, OREGON – 1968

No matter where the world said she should be or what she should be doing, Barbie Rose was happiest on the back of a horse. Especially on a day as beautiful and full of promise as the one she'd woken up to that morning. She'd smiled so much while driving her Volkswagen Beetle to work at the Langley's Legacy Ranch that every time she stopped at a red light, someone grinned back at her. Although that could have been because they too knew that it was a special day. It wasn't until she'd parked outside of the Langley's stable and gone in to start her daily tasks that she'd felt at home, though.

"Are you excited, girl?" she asked Daisy as the horse pulled against her reins.

Daisy wanted to run, but their work that morning had involved riding out to check fences around the perimeter of the property. Boring, but necessary. Mr. Aidan Langley, the ranch's current owner, had requested that Barbie put together a report of all the maintenance that needed doing on the ranch, along with a recommendation of how the work should be done and who among the ranch hands should do it. Desk work wasn't her favorite thing to do, but since Mr. Langley had retired, hiring her to do the bulk of the managerial work on the ranch, her drive to make him proud was just about as strong as her need to prove herself to the men she worked with. Correct that, the men who worked for her. Men who weren't used to seeing a woman somewhere other than in the kitchen, wearing an apron, much less giving them orders.

"Oh boy, you really do want to run," she laughed as Daisy stepped restlessly to the side. "Or are you just excited about Heath coming home?"

Just saying the words sent a ripple of excitement through her. At last, the day the entire Langley family had been waiting for, the day New Dawn Springs had been hoping for, had come. Heath

Langley had served his time in Vietnam and was coming home today.

"All right, go." Barbie gave up trying to hold Daisy back and tapped her sides. In an instant, the horse shot off across the large, enclosed field where several of the other Langley horses grazed or frolicked in the morning sun. Daisy ran with her heart on her sleeve, obviously loving every moment as her muscles worked and the wind streamed across her sleek, chestnut body.

Barbie loved the run as much as Daisy did, but it was Heath who had her heart singing. No one had been surprised two years ago when Heath and Davy Sudgeon enlisted. The two of them had talked of nothing but doing their duty and serving their country all through high school, when they and Barbie were inseparable. At their parents' insistence, they'd delayed enlisting until after college, but almost as soon as Heath and Davy had walked across the stage at the University of Oregon, they'd kept walking, all the way to the Army recruitment office.

It had been the worst day of Barbie's life. She'd watched the war reports on CBS every night, and even though President Johnson continued to insist everything was going well in Vietnam and that victory was only a year or so away, the images on tv told a different story. She'd chewed her nails to the quick any time images of bombs exploding in sultry jungles were broadcast, and breathed only temporary sighs of relief when reports that the Viet Cong had lost more troops than the Americans were discussed.

To her, the war wasn't just about statistics and far-off jungles. Heath and Davy had been her closest friends through all the years when the girls her age had written her off as a hopeless tomboy. The other girls had gone crazy over the new mini-skirt fashions, make-up, and Elvis, but she'd been more interested in horses, studying veterinary medicine, and securing a job she could be proud of.

But right at the end of college, just as she was beginning to despair that not a single ranch in Oregon would hire a woman to run their operations, and as Heath and Davy had gotten closer to enlisting, things between her and Heath had heated up. The night before he left for basic training, the two of them had shared a kiss that had knocked her socks off and made her reconsider her disdain for the domestic life of her mother's generation.

And then he was gone. For two years, Barbie had had nothing but letters from Heath. Those had grown fewer and further between. Then came the

Battle of Khe Sahn. Two official communications were sent home to New Dawn Springs. One informed the Langleys that Heath had been wounded in battle. The other was to tell the Sudgeons that Davy had been killed in action. Barbie had only received one letter from Heath since then—a short note written from his hospital bed saying that he wasn't reenlisting when his tour was over.

Barbie shook herself out of her thoughts as Daisy made a turn. Her smile had vanished, and the pain she still felt for Davy's loss rippled through her. "Easy girl," she told Daisy. "Where are you going?"

The answer was obvious. Daisy was headed straight for the barrel course that took up one side of the corral on the west side of the Langley's extensive stable. Barbie's smile returned.

"Really, girl? You want to race? Well, go on, then."

Daisy's focus was absolute as she shot onto the course and headed for the first barrel. She hadn't been trained for racing. She hadn't been trained for anything. Daisy was Davy's horse. She'd been boarded with the Langleys her entire life, but Davy's whole world had revolved around her since the day she was born. Everyone had been certain Daisy wouldn't make it, but Davy had had faith in her.

He'd headed off to war before she'd had a chance to develop into the brilliant horse she was. Barbie was the one who discovered she had a yearning to run.

"Good girl," Barbie panted as Daisy pulled around the first barrel and shot off toward the second. There was still work to do. Daisy's desire needed to be honed into skill, but the basics were there. They rounded the second barrel easily and headed to the third. No one had ever dreamed that a horse who had nearly died during birth would be nimble enough to race, but Daisy wasn't about to quit. "Go, girl, go," Barbie shouted as they rounded the last barrel.

It was a clumsy turn, but Daisy made it without falling. Barbie gripped the saddle tightly with her legs, leaned low over Daisy's neck, and made a beeline for the stable. She pulled up just before they reached it, bringing Daisy to a stop. Daisy snorted and bobbed her head. Barbie could feel the exhilaration radiating from her.

"That was some fine racing."

Barbie sucked in a breath and turned in the saddle to find Aidan Langley watching her from the side of the corral. He leaned against the fence, his grey hair tousled by the June breeze. The lines around his eyes betrayed years of smiling, and even though he was in his sixties and weathered, he had the vibrancy of a much younger man.

"Hi, Mr. Langley," Barbie greeted him, panting. She pulled Daisy around and walked her to the edge of the fence. "Shouldn't you be up at the house waiting for Heath?"

A wide smile spread across Aidan's face. "Couldn't sit still," he confessed. "Thought I'd come down here and see how you're getting along."

"I just got back from checking the fences." A flash of self-consciousness pricked at Barbie. She hoped Aidan didn't think she'd been playing around instead of working. It was hard enough to convince the other stable hands she was serious about her work. Everything depended on Aidan Langley approving of her. "Daisy here just wanted to race." She patted Daisy's neck.

Aidan chuckled. "I could see that." His expression pinched. "You don't think you're pushing her too hard, are you? She's always been a bit delicate."

"Daisy?" Barbie dismounted, hopping to the ground. She came around to rub Daisy's nose. "Nah. This girl's much stronger than anyone gives her credit for."

"Are you sure?" Aidan asked. "She had such a rough start."

"That was years ago." Barbie kept her tone light and spoke more to Daisy than Aidan. It grated on her nerves that everyone underestimated not only Daisy, but her too. A flicker of movement caught her eye, and she glanced up to see Rick, a middle-aged man who had been working in the Langley stables for years, coming out to the paddock. "Hey, Rick, could you come take Daisy from me? She needs a good rub-down."

Rick stopped mid-step and frowned. "I've got work to do," he said, though the pack of cigarettes in his hand and the fact that he was heading away from the stable said otherwise.

Barbie's chest tightened. "I need you to take care of Daisy."

"Can't you do it?" Rick asked.

Aidan turned to him. "Rick, Barbie here is your boss. You'd best do what she says."

Rick's scowl deepened, but he tucked his pack of cigarettes into his back pocket and walked over to take Daisy's reins. He didn't say a word, but resentment dripped off him as he led Daisy back to the stable. Barbie watched him until he disappeared into the building, an anxious knot in her stomach.

"How are things going down here?" Aidan asked.

Barbie clenched her teeth for a moment, then turned to him. "About like you'd expect."

Aidan chuckled. "That bad, eh?"

Barbie sighed. "Men are going to have to get used to having female bosses." She swiped the wide-brimmed hat from her head and wiped her forehead on her sleeve. "I wasn't the only woman in my college classes. More and more of us are getting out there in the workforce. If you ask me, we're on the cusp of a sea-change."

"You don't need to tell me." Aidan held up his hands. "Rick'll come around," he went on. "Let me know if he doesn't."

"I will, sir."

"I'm more concerned about what I just saw out there." He nodded to the barrel course.

Barbie winced. "I should have told you Daisy's been in a racing mood lately. She really is a natural. I've actually been thinking of entering her in an amateur competition to see how she'd do."

"You think Marge and Robert would allow it?"

Barbie bit her lip and stared at the course. Davy's parents didn't know she'd begun training Daisy to race. Almost immediately after word of his loss had reached them, they'd come down to the stable and spent hours just hugging and stroking Daisy, as though she were all they had left of their only child. They'd come by a lot since then, bringing Daisy treats. Marge Sudgeon asked Barbie how Daisy was doing every time they crossed paths in town.

"I think if they could see how much Daisy loves racing they'd be fine with it," she said at last. She paused, kicked the ground, and bit her lip before glancing up to Aidan again. "She's not the same fragile foal she was, Mr. Langley. And we can't treat her like she's made out of glass just because Davy's gone."

A sad look came over Aidan that put years on his face. He sighed and opened his mouth to speak, but the beep of a horn cut his words off. He and Barbie both glanced down the drive to see a worn, blue truck driving toward the house, a cloud of dust kicking up behind it.

Barbie's heart sped up, and her breath caught in her lungs. "Is that them?" she asked.

Aidan didn't answer. He was already rushing toward the house.

HOME. HEATH DREW IN A LONG BREATH OF fresh, country air as Chip, his brother-in-law, drove through the gate and up the long, gravel drive. It was a warm day, but after the sweltering heat and humidity of the Vietnamese highlands, after days spent fording muddy rivers while mosquitoes flew so thick you couldn't help but breathe them in, and where the incessant drone of insects was broken only by the rhythmic drumming of rain, or worse, explosions, he'd take a little Pacific Northwestern heat.

"Things haven't changed much since you left," Chip said, smiling, his tone conversational. "You haven't been gone long enough for much to happen."

"Yeah," Heath said, agreeing because the truth was too big to comprehend.

Everything had changed. The world had expanded overnight from the dozy, rural paradise of home, to the vast, smoldering, incomprehensible world. He'd changed right along with it.

"Other than the fact that Rachel had another baby, we've all just been rolling along," Chip went on.

"It'll be nice to meet my new niece," Heath said. It was the answer Chip was looking for.

"And, well, I guess you could say that your dad hiring Barbara Rose to run the day-to-day business of the ranch is a big change."

Heath's heart squeezed a little harder at the mention of Barbie. Fondness and expectation warred with guilt in his gut. He should have written more. He should have explained things. Especially since Barbie had been in his thoughts almost constantly on those long, steamy, terrifying nights.

"I'm back now," he said, glancing out at the stable down the hill as they grew closer to the house. The building was as familiar to him as the back of his hand, and the horses that wandered the fields and corrals around it were like siblings and cousins to him. He strained his eyes looking to see if Daisy was out with the rest of the bunch.

Thoughts of Daisy inevitably brought thoughts of Davy, of his laugh and his smile, the size of his eyes when they'd hopped down from the truck at their first assignment near Saigon. Those memories swiftly faded to the fear in his eyes on night patrol, the hollow look in his face as he lost weight. The way he'd closed his eyes and let go even as Heath put everything he had into dragging his wounded body to safety.

Heath sucked in a breath, shaking himself.

"You all right there?" Chip asked.

"Yeah, I'm fine."

Heath reached into his pocket, pulling out the

antique pocket watch that had helped him make it through his tour of duty. He traced his thumb over the clover pattern on the cover. His dad had given him the watch when he left for basic training, making him swear that he'd bring it home. The watch had worked then. He hadn't thought much of it at first, and had kept it in his locker during basic. He'd moved it to his pocket once they'd reached Vietnam to keep it from being stolen. After his first battle, he'd taken to holding it in quiet moments, feeling the steady tick against his palm. It had stopped working after a particularly bad night, spent waist-deep in a swamp, but he'd still taken it out every night and traced the design on the front. After Khe Sahn, after Davy, it had been the only thing holding him to sanity during his time in the military hospital.

Chip made a disapproving sound as he turned the truck into a parking spot along with half a dozen other cars and trucks. "I told them you wouldn't want any sort of display like that."

Heath glanced up from the watch to find his whole extended family lined up on the porch. His mom stood near the center, face hidden in her hands, as his oldest sister, Kathy, hugged her from the side. Her twin, his brother Kevin, hadn't been able to get away from his job in Dallas to join the reunion, but would be there for the Fourth of July. His three other sisters, Colleen, Kelly, and Rachel, stood on the porch steps with their kids around them. His nephews, Brandon and Kyle, held a hand-painted sign that read "Welcome home, Hero".

Heath clenched his jaw, pain radiating from his heart. He wasn't a hero. He'd done his duty. Davy was the hero. He was the one who would never come home. But the gesture was well-meant. He swallowed several times to keep the bile from rising up his throat. He had no right to be bitter, not really.

"Here you go," Chip said, cutting the truck's engine. "I'll take care of your things. You greet your family."

Heath nodded, then tucked the watch back in his pocket before opening the door and hopping down. His injured leg threatened to give way for a moment, but he steadied himself, gripping the door, glad that his mom was on the other side of the truck. The bullets he'd taken in his thigh had been a minor inconvenience, compared to some of the wounds his fellow soldiers had suffered, but he figured he'd have to be careful for the rest of his life. In more ways than one. At least he still had his leg, and his life.

He took a deep breath, steadying himself for

what would inevitably come next. Home was home, and it was beyond wonderful to be there, but he knew that his family was about to look at him and see someone who wasn't there anymore. It would take time for them to come to grips with the man he was now. Hell, it would take time for *him* to come to grips with his new self.

He plastered on a smile and walked around the back of the truck, heading for the porch. The first thing he noticed was that his dad wasn't there. Neither was the other person he'd been hoping and praying would be there to greet him. He and Barbie had left so much unsaid when he'd left. So much had been left out of their letters too.

"Heath. Oh, my baby boy. I'm so glad you're home." His mom broke away from the rest of the family, charging down the porch steps, and running across the yard to him. Tears streaked her face.

Heath caught her when she reached him, hugging her so tight he was afraid he'd break her. "Ma. It's so good to see you again."

All at once, he was the little boy in overalls, bandages on both knees and both elbows, that he'd once been. He didn't care how old he got or how much of the world he'd seen, his mom would always be his mom.

Once the floodgates were open, everyone rushed forward to meet him. Each of his sisters hugged him in turn, their husbands shook his hand, and the kids either hugged him or glanced up in awe at the uncle they barely remembered.

"Why aren't you wearing your uniform?" his mom asked, never letting go of him, even as everyone else tried to hug him.

"I changed at the airport in Portland," he said, making light of what had been a difficult but important decision for him. He'd wanted to truly come home, to leave the nightmare of his service behind him, as soon as possible. He *wanted* to leave it behind, but suspected he never would. "Where's Pa?" he asked, glancing around.

"He's down by the stable," Kathleen said.

"He couldn't sit still while waiting for you," his mom said. "So he went to check on Barbie and the horses."

"Barbie's here?" His heart leapt in his chest.

"She works here now," Rachel said. "Didn't Pa write to you to say?"

"He did. Barbie wrote too." He twisted in the middle of the crowd of family hugging him to glance down toward the stable. His father was making his way up the hill, but he had a long way to go. "Excuse me just a sec," he said, peeling away from the others.

"Let him go," his mom said as he headed toward the stable with long strides.

Beyond his father, Barbie stood near the fenced corral. Her short, black hair framed her face, and though he was too far away to see her features clearly, he would know her a mile away. He remembered the way she'd always laughed at his stupid jokes, the way she'd helped him study in high school. And he remembered the way her lips had tasted when he'd kissed her goodbye. He'd been waiting to go home, waiting to see the people he loved most, almost from the day he'd left for basic, but he'd been waiting to hold Barbie again more than anything.

## 2

Barbie's heart felt like it wanted to jump right out of her chest as she watched Heath pull away from his family and start down the hill toward the stable. There was a slight hitch in his walk which had to be the remnant of the injury he'd had back in January, but it barely slowed him down. Heath had to be itching to hug his dad. Aidan was marching up the hill as fast as he could, after all. But a little part of her hoped that he wanted to see her as well. She took a step forward, hesitated, danced to the side...then laughed at herself.

"I'm as jumpy as Daisy," she murmured.

She drew in a breath, then headed up the hill. Heath and his dad met and threw their arms around each other in a bear-hug that made Barbie's throat squeeze and tears come to her eyes. She couldn't imagine how wonderful it must be to greet your father after being away at war. Her dad had served in the Pacific twenty-five years ago, but he rarely talked about his experiences. Then again, he rarely talked about anything.

Thoughts of her dad flew out of her head as she approached Heath and Aidan. Her heart beat faster, and, even though it was crazy, her lips tingled as though Heath had kissed her two seconds ago instead of two years. When he let go of his dad and looked at her, and she couldn't hold back.

"You're home," she cried, running toward him.

"Barbie." Heath didn't have time to say more as she threw herself into his arms.

Heath stumbled a little more than Barbie thought he would have before, but as soon as his arms went around her, she knew everything would be okay. His body was warm, and his familiar scent filled her as she breathed him in. She'd missed the way he smelled. She hummed with joy and rested her head against his for a moment before kissing his cheek—wishing she were bold enough to do more—and stepping back.

"You look fantastic," she said, raking him with an appreciative glance.

"Thanks," he answered, the slightest hint of

disagreement in his expression. That pinched look faded as he studied her. "You look great yourself. When did you cut your hair?"

Barbie raised a hand to her bob. "Not long after you left, actually. I figured I needed something that looked professional, since your dad hired me to manage the stable here."

"I'm so proud of you for that."

"Barbie here has done a fine job of running things," Aidan said, patting Barbie on the back.

Heath smiled. "Thanks for keeping an eye on things while I was gone."

An uncomfortable hitch formed in Barbie's gut. "Not just while you were gone. This is my job now."

A momentary frown creased Heath's brow, but it vanished before Barbie was certain she'd seen it.

"Heath, are you going to come inside and tell us all about your journey home?" Maura called from slightly farther up the hill as she walked toward them.

Barbie glanced past her to see the rest of the family heading onto the porch and into the house.

Heath turned to give his mom a smile, but it didn't reach his eyes. "Yeah, Ma. I'll be there in just a second. I want to see how the horses are doing first."

Maura grinned as if she knew better. "Barbie,

you're welcome to join us." Her brow twitched slightly as she glanced to her.

"Thanks, Mrs. Langley. Let me just see what needs doing in the stables," Barbie said.

Aidan patted her shoulder again. "That's our Barbie. Always on top of things. You should get her to show you how she's organized all the invoices and order forms."

"Paperwork?" Heath's brow inched up, half in amusement, half in a sort of relief that irked Barbie, though she couldn't explain why.

"You don't want to see paperwork," she said, crossing her arms. She told herself the gesture wasn't defensive, wasn't confrontational. It was just comfortable.

"Why don't I leave the two of you alone while I go help your mom." Aidan winked at Barbie, then marched past them up the hill.

Barbie glanced to Heath, her cheeks heating. "You didn't, uh, write all sorts of things home to them, did you? Like, about the way we said goodbye when you left?"

A teasing, tantalizing look flashed into Heath's eyes. "There's no way I'd write to my parents about that."

A giggle escaped from Barbie before she could

stop it. She clapped a hand to her mouth before turning and walking by Heath's side toward the stable.

"So how bad was your injury?" she asked, glancing down to his leg as they walked.

Heath's smile vanished so fast that Barbie's stomach lurched. "It's fine."

She pressed her lips shut. He was lying. Well, maybe not lying exactly, but his response was clearly designed to shut down any further questions. The whole thing had happened so fast that instinct told her Heath's wounds were worse than she'd imagined. Not his physical wounds either. She'd seen more than a few Vietnam vets coming home damaged. They all knew someone who knew a vet who'd fallen into depression, gotten wrapped up in drugs, or worse.

"You don't have to talk about it if you don't want to," she said as they stepped through the open stable door and into the long, dimmer room.

"There's nothing to talk about," Heath snapped.

Barbie hesitated as they walked past the first line of stalls. The scent of hay, horse, and manure was a familiar comfort. "You don't have to pretend with me, Heath," she said quietly, then added before he could contradict her, "But I won't ask about anything if you don't want me to."

Heath remained silent. His jaw was clenched, and he kept his eyes straight forward. It was almost as if he hadn't heard what she'd said, though clearly he had. He let out a breath as they turned the corner to the newer part of the stable—a second section of stalls that had been built just ten years before. Barbie knew exactly where he was headed, and wasn't surprised at all.

"Hey, Daisy." Heath greeted Davy's horse with a soft voice, reaching out to stroke her nose as they reached her stall.

Daisy blew out a soft breath and stepped forward, leaning into Heath's shoulder. It was obvious that she remembered him. Heath lowered his head, resting his forehead against the top of Daisy's head and closing his eyes. Barbie swallowed hard, her heart breaking and her thoughts flying straight to Davy and what he would have made of this homecoming. Davy's absence was so palpable that it was as if he were standing there with them, paradoxical as it was.

"I'm trying to work here." Rick's grouchy voice pierced through the moment as he stood in the back of the stall. He must have just been finishing up currying Daisy, as he still had the brush in his hand. The moment he spotted Heath, his scowl melted into a smile. "Heath. It's good to see you home again."

"Hey, Rick." Heath let go of Daisy and stepped back, clearing his throat as though he'd been caught kissing a girl. "It's good to be home."

Rick let himself out of the stall, tossing the currying brush in a barrel as he went, then came over to slap Heath on the back. "You kill a lot of VC while you were over there?"

The color drained from Heath's face so fast Barbie thought she would have to catch him when he passed out.

Instead, Heath let out a nervous laugh. "Yeah."

"Don't you have something you're meant to be doing?" Barbie narrowed her eyes at Rick.

Rick stared back at her, his eyes wide, then turned to Heath. "It's a good thing you're back. This chick has been getting ahead of herself."

"Excuse me?" Barbie crossed her arms.

"See what I mean?" Rick shook his head. "Chick bosses. Worst idea ever. Hey, man. I'm sorry about Davy."

The conversation shifted so fast that Barbie didn't know what to say. She was ready to string Rick up by his entrails, but calling him out when he'd apologized for Davy made the timing all wrong.

"Thanks," Heath said, his voice hoarse.

"It'll be groovy to see you back at work soon," Rick said, thumping Heath on the back, then walking away. He glanced over his shoulder and said, "Why don't you marry that one and knock her up so she quits messing with us?" He laughed as if he'd made a joke, then disappeared around the corner.

Barbie was so offended she was surprised smoke wasn't coming out her ears.

"Want me to talk to Dad about firing him?" Heath asked.

"No," Barbie snapped, more upset that he would offer to solve her problems for her than she was irritated by Rick. "I can deal with it. I've been dealing with it for over a year."

"All right, all right." Heath held his hands up. A moment later, he let out a breath that turned into a laugh.

"What's that for?"

He shook his head. "I just spent two years in a war-zone, and it looks like I came back to another one."

Guilt washed through Barbie. "I'm sorry." She

dropped her shoulders and her angry energy drained with it.

"No, no," Heath protested, reaching into the stall to stroke Daisy's neck. "I missed this kind of thing."

Barbie arched a brow. "What, Rick being a misogynistic bastard and giving me a hard time?"

"No, and I'm sorry about that," Heath said. He let out a breath. "I missed normal."

The last of Barbie's anger melted away. She stepped into Heath, hugging him. "I know you don't want to talk about it, but I'm here if you ever find you need to."

Heath stiffened in her embrace, tension rippling from him. Barbie let go just as that tension began to subside. She instantly wished she'd held him longer, but then again, they weren't dating. No promises had been made before Heath and Davy left. All they had was that kiss.

"We'd better get up to the house before your mom comes looking for us," Barbie said, stoking Daisy's nose before stepping away from the stall. She shouldn't feel so awkward around a guy she'd known since she was a kid, a guy she loved in more ways than one. But instinct told her the Heath standing in front of her now had been through so much that she'd have to get to know him all over again.

"Yeah," he agreed, following her down the row, around the corner, and out into the sunshine again. "Sorry about Ma. I'm the only one of her kids who isn't married, and you know she's always liked you."

Barbie laughed. "As far back as I can remember, people have always assumed I'd end up with either Davy or you. I guess now—"

She stopped, almost missing a step. Guilt hit her so fast it nearly took her breath away. Heath's steps slowed beside her, and, for a second, she thought he was going to have to stop. His face had gone downright ashen.

She swallowed, working some moisture into her suddenly try throat. "Were you...were you with him when he...."

Heath nodded. His eyes took on a haunted, glassy look. A rush of panic hit her. Heath had always been strong, cocky, even. She didn't know what she'd do if he broke down.

"I'm sorry," she whispered.

They were halfway up the hill before he shook his head and sucked in a breath. "I'll talk to Dad about Rick first thing tomorrow. You shouldn't have to put up with that kind of behavior."

Barbie nodded slowly, frowning. If he didn't want to talk about Davy, she could respect that. But she wasn't comfortable with him stepping in on her problems either. "It's okay."

They were silent the rest of the way to the house, but the silence didn't last long. The second they were through the doors, noise erupted everywhere. Maura had cooked a feast, which was spread out over the dining room table. All of Heath's sisters seemed to be helping at once and getting in each other's way. Their husbands were trying to fill plates for themselves and their kids as new dishes were added to the table. The tv blared in the other room as the kids watched Bonanza, and the Langleys' dog, Jackson—whose name was a family inside joke—barked and tried to get to the table.

"Well, you said you wanted normal," Barbie said, leaning closer to Heath.

"This is perfect," he replied, heading toward the table. "Ma, this looks great," he said as he started fixing a plate.

"I made all your favorites," Maura said. "Fried chicken, creamed spinach, those mashed potatoes with the onions you like."

Heath loaded a large scoop of potatoes on his plate. "It looks delicious."

"And for desert there's—"

Gunshots sounded from the tv, and all at once,

Heath dropped his plate and lurched back. The plate hit the side of the table, then shattered on the floor. Barbie grabbed Heath's arm to steady him, not knowing what else to do.

"Change the channel, change the channel," Kathleen hissed, leaping over kids and toys to reach the tv set in the corner. She turned the dial, and the cute, perky music and laugh track of *The Flying Nun* replaced the gunfire.

"I'll clean it up," Rachel whispered, her face pale, as she rushed to pick up the pieces of Heath's shattered plate.

"I can do it," Heath said, kneeling by her side. "You've just had a baby. You shouldn't have to do any of this."

"No, but—"

"I insist."

Rachel stood slowly, sending Barbie a look of panic. The only thing Barbie could think to do was to rest a hand on Rachel's arm and nod. The entire family had gone silent, watching as Heath picked up after himself.

"I'll get the dustpan," Maura said at last, dashing into the kitchen.

Colleen ran after her, eventually returning on

her own with the dustpan. Aidan slipped quietly into the kitchen.

"Step back and let Jackson clean up the potatoes," Chip said at last. "It's about time a Jackson did their share of the work around here."

The others laughed—far louder than the weak joke deserved. But at least the moment of tension was broken. Heath finished cleaning up his mess, and Rachel took the dustpan into the kitchen.

"I'm sure it'll get better," Barbie whispered as Heath started fixing himself another plate.

His only answer was to raise a doubtful eyebrow.

"Your father tells me this is the perfect occasion to open that bottle of wine Henry and April gave us for Christmas," Maura announced with an over-cheery smile as she and Aidan swept back into the room. "Although I would rather save it for your coming home party," she told Heath, coming over to him and kissing his cheek.

Barbie felt a little like an intruder as Maura's expression turned apologetic and Heath looked back at her with reassurance. Some communication should only be between parents and children, but neither seemed to mind that she was standing right there, witnessing it.

"Wine sounds great, Ma," Heath said, taking the

bottle from her with his free hand. "I'm not so sure about a party, though."

"Of course we'll have a party," Kathleen spoke up. She came over to take Heath's plate, loading it with goodies as Heath moved to the antique cupboard on one side of the room, presumably to look for a corkscrew. "Everybody loves parties."

Just like that, the room returned to normal. The kids stopped looking as though they were walking on eggshells and went back to watching tv, Heath's sisters returned to fussing with food and plates, and their husbands continued the conversation about who they thought would be most competitive in the rodeo coming up after the Fourth of July.

"Oh, that reminds me," Barbie said, moving to help Heath with wine glasses as Kathleen and Maura continued talking about the party. "I was telling your dad earlier, I think I'm going to enter Daisy in the barrel races at the rodeo next month."

Heath stared at her as though she'd dropped the glasses in her hands. "You're what?"

"Daisy has taken to running the barrels," Barbie explained with a shrug, carrying the glasses to the table as Heath set to work uncorking the bottle. "She watched some of the other horses running the course and wanted to give it a try herself one day."

Heath shook his head. "Horses don't make up their minds to do things like that." Barbie was set to disagree with him, but he went on with, "And besides, Daisy is much too delicate for something as strenuous as racing. She might get hurt."

"She's not delicate at all. She's grown a lot since you and Davy left."

Heath's expression hardened. "She might get hurt. Davy wouldn't want that."

"I think he would."

"Well, he wouldn't." Heath popped the cork from the wine and brought the conversation to an end so thoroughly that everyone else stopped talking for a moment to look at him. Heath seemed to notice. He cleared his throat and glanced to his sisters, then his mother. "A party sounds like a great idea," he said.

"We can have it next week." Maura jumped right in, crossing to take the uncorked bottle of wine from him. "You won't have to worry about a thing. I'll take care of everything." Her look was so careful, so much like a mother protecting her son, that heat rushed to Barbie's face.

"Thanks, Ma," Heath mumbled, then looked around. "What happened to my plate? I'm starving, and I haven't had a home-cooked meal in ages."

"It's right here," Kathleen said, her smile a little too wide, returning Heath's plate. "Barbie, do you want me to fix something for you too?"

"No, I've got it," Barbie said.

She headed to the other end of the table where the fried chicken sat and helped herself, but her attention stayed focused on Heath. The party might not have been a great idea. It was plain as day that Heath had a lot of adjusting to do. She didn't know if the Army offered any kind of counseling for vets who had lost friends, or lost themselves, but she could see Heath needed something. She promised herself that she'd be there for him, whatever it took. But she thought of Daisy, she thought of the things Rick had said in the stable. Everything was an uphill battle. She would be there for Heath, but not if it meant giving up her own dreams.

3

*A* few day's rest. That was all Heath needed. Or so he convinced himself. He only flinched at the gunfire on tv because he was tired and overwhelmed after finally getting home. All he needed was his mom's cooking, a few nights of deep, dreamless sleep in his old bed, and life to return to normal. He'd return to normal too.

It sounded simple enough, but as he headed down to the stables three days after his homecoming, tension continued to sit on his shoulders like a gremlin. He hadn't dreamed about Davy for three nights, hadn't had flashes of that swamp, the bombs exploding, and the high-pitched, screaming bullets that whizzed past them. He hadn't dreamed about the moment the sniper's bullet pierced Davy's throat or the horror in his best friend's eyes as he realized he was dead. No, those memories only hit him when he was awake.

He needed normal. He needed work and distraction. He needed the throbbing ache of his own, recovering leg as he marched down the hill to the stable, paradoxical as that was. Everything would be fine once he got back to work.

"Boy, am I glad to see you here," Rick greeted him as he approached the stable door.

"Hey, Rick." Heath waved.

Rick snorted and nodded at the VW Beetle parked beside three other dirty, rusty trucks behind the stable. "Get a load of that. That chick doesn't have a clue."

Heath glanced at Barbie's car, unable to keep the smile off his face. Barbie had gotten her license way before him or Davy, and for a year or so, she'd been their chief source of transportation. He'd gone on more than a few wild adventures in that silly car.

He didn't respond to Rick's jab before stepping into the stable and breathing in the scent of home. "This is more like it," he sighed, closing his eyes for a minute.

"It'll be even more like it once you send that woman packing," Rick muttered as he entered the stable and marched past Heath.

Heath frowned, but rather than catching Rick and asking him to stop, he headed for the stable office.

Sure enough, Barbie sat at his dad's old desk, jotting things down in the ranch ledger. He knocked on the doorframe, and when she looked up, a smile lit up her face.

"Heath. What brings you here so bright and early?" She leaned back in her chair, tapping the eraser of her pencil against her lips.

The simple motion sent fire through Heath's blood. The burst of normal, human wanting was so soothing that he didn't even try to hide his body's reaction or the look he was pretty sure came into his eyes. "I'm here to work," he said instead, shrugging.

A flash of tension pulled the muscles of Barbie's pretty face tight. She hesitated before saying, "You know I'm in charge now, right?"

Prickles popped up on Heath's back. He supposed even that was a welcome part of normal, but he didn't relish the idea of competing with Barbie to get his job back. "I'm sure there's plenty I can do around here."

"I'm sure." She tossed her pencil down and stood. Barbie had been petite enough to pass for a pixie when they were growing up, but she'd shot up when they were teens, and was now only a few inches shorter than him. Her short hair and sharp bangs didn't exactly make her look like a boy—with curves like hers, Barbie would never look like a boy—but as she stepped around the desk to face him with crossed arms, she was as formidable as any ranch hand. "So what are you looking to do?"

Heath shrugged. "I've done all the business work of the ranch in the past, so obviously, I know how to order feed, medicine, and supplies."

"That's my job now." She stared at him with rock-solid confidence.

"I used to go around and inspect all the horses each morning to make sure they're all in top shape."

"Already done, first thing. I've got a system now and ledgers to track it."

Heath paused, frowning. He shifted his stance, crossing his arms. "Are there any concerns I should know about?"

She chewed her lip and stared at nothing for a second, as if debating what to say. "Lady Bird is getting up there, and we're concerned that age is catching up with her. Bentley stepped on a sharp rock last week, and he's not healing as fast as we would like. Erie had an infection after foaling that she can't seem to shake, and we're keeping an eye on her foal, since she seems to be having a bad start."

"Kind of like Daisy?" Heath's eyebrows inched up. Images of Davy clinging to him as Heath dragged him out of the swamp flashed to his mind.

Barbie frowned. "Daisy isn't the fragile baby she once was. She has the heart of a champion."

"I'm sure she does. She's Davy's horse."

Silence fell between them. Heath couldn't imagine what he looked like, but the way Barbie's frown melted into a sympathetic look gave him a hint.

"There has to be something I can do," he went on, wanting to see anything but pity from her.

She nodded to his leg. "How much *can* you do? What has your leg left you capable of?"

"Man, you don't pull any punches, do you?" he laughed, not sure whether he liked that she wasn't coddling him or hated that she pointed out his weakness so easily.

She shrugged and walked toward him. "You say you want something to do, but most of the stuff that needs doing around here requires a lot of strength. I don't want you to push yourself if you're not done healing yet."

"I've healed up enough," he said, following her as

she marched out into the rows of stalls. He hoped it was true.

"Okay, then why don't you help me get some of these babies out into the corral and bring out a few hay bales. They'll probably wander out to graze closer to the meadow, but I like to make sure the older ones don't have to go far for a meal."

"Whatever you say."

She glanced over her shoulder, grinning at him. "I like the sound of that."

Her grin sent a burst of longing through him that reminded him of their last kiss. What a night that had been. The two of them and Davy had gone out for a night on the town. He'd driven for a change, and after he'd taken Davy home, he and Barbie had gone for a walk around the ranch. He'd told her all about his hopes and fears, and when they reached the old oak at the far end of the meadow, with the light of the full moon shining down, he'd kissed her. It had started out simple, but in no time her back was against the tree, his hand was under her sweater, and their tongues were dueling in the best way possible. It had been a taste of heaven right before two years in hell.

"Here we go," Barbie said in a sweet voice as she

approached a stall with a dappled grey mare. "You ready for the sun, Cherry?"

The mare snorted and came to the front of the stall as if she knew the routine. Heath walked over to stroke her neck, keeping most of his attention on Barbie. She moved as though she not only knew what she was doing, but as though it were in her blood. Which was funny, considering her dad was an accountant and her mom a homemaker.

"There you go," she said, unlatching the stall and opening the door. "Heath here will escort you out, lucky girl."

Heath laughed and moved to lead Cherry out toward the paddock as Barbie moved down the aisle to check on another horse. A sense of calm filled Heath.

"Oh, Heath. I'm glad you're here." Oliver, one of the other ranch hands who had worked for his family since before he left, marched around the corner from the second row of stalls.

"Hey, Ollie. What's up?"

"I was wondering if you'd had a chance to look at Lady Bird yet." Ollie launched right into things. "She doesn't want to eat this morning, and I thought—"

"What are you doing?" Barbie stepped out of the

stall she'd ducked into, planting her hands on her hips.

Ollie glanced from her to Heath and back again. "I'm trying to figure out what to do about Lady Bird."

Barbie started forward. "We have a protocol for Lady Bird," she said. "We talked about this last week."

"Yeah, but with Heath home...." Ollie gestured to Heath with his thumb.

Uneasiness rippled down Heath's spine. "I can take a look at her after I get this one out to the paddock," he said. "Lady Bird might just need time. She hasn't been sick or anything lately, has she?"

"No," Ollie said.

"I have this handled," Barbie insisted, striding forward, an incredulous look in her eyes. She turned to Ollie. "I'll come take a look at her as soon as I finish with Lancer."

"Yeah, but," Ollie started. He glanced to Heath. "He's here now."

Barbie crossed her arms. "That doesn't change the job I was hired to do."

A dubious look passed across Ollie's face. He shook his head, glanced significantly to Heath one last time, then marched off.

"I'll thank you not to go undermining my

authority like that," Barbie growled, closing the distance between them. "I know none of these guys are used to having a female boss, but that's the way things are now, whether you're back or not."

Several thoughts zipped through Heath's mind at once. The guys didn't like being bossed around by a woman, and that wasn't likely to change any time soon. Barbie had enough fire in her to run a dozen ranches. And she was downright gorgeous when she was angry. He remembered that tree, remembered the way she'd sighed as they kissed.

He cleared his throat. "Why don't I get Cherry out to the paddock and we can discuss this more."

"There's nothing to discuss," she fired back, then turned and marched back to the stall she'd been in before.

Heath waited until she led out one of the Langley's signature appaloosas, and they walked out to the paddock together. Half a dozen horses were already grazing or walking with each other in the warm, June morning. Cherry and the appaloosa trotted off to join them. Heath paused to watch them for a moment before peeking at Barbie.

"I'm not giving up my job just because you came back from the war," she said, arms crossed, frowning at the horses ambling toward the far end of the paddock.

"I didn't ask you to," Heath replied. He caught sight of Daisy among the other horses. His heart lurched in his chest. She looked good in the sunlight, breaking away from the others to run for a moment. Davy would have been proud of her.

Still frowning, Barbie turned to him. "I worked hard to get where I am. Harder than any man has to work. And I know that my mother's generation all gave up their jobs and popped out babies when the G.I.s came home from Germany and the Pacific, but times have changed."

"I never asked you to give up your job to keep house and raise babies," Heath said. Although he wouldn't lie and say the image of her doing just that didn't intrigue him. Making those babies most of all.

"It hasn't been easy," she said, almost too quiet to be heard, glancing out over the paddock again.

"If it's not easy, why do it?" he asked.

She turned back to him, gaping as though he'd kicked a puppy. "This is what I want to do. Ever since I first started spending time with you and Davy on this ranch. Ever since your dad taught me to ride. All I've wanted to do is take care of horses. And I'm good at it too."

"I'm sure you are."

"And I'm sick and tired of you pricks telling me I can't do as good a job as you just because I have tits."

Heath's eyes popped open. He would have expected that kind of language in the Army, but not from cute, fiery Barbie. The world really *had* changed.

Barbie stepped away from him, raising her hands to her mouth and whistling long and loud. At the other end of the paddock, Daisy raised her head, then left what she'd been doing to run home to Barbie.

"Wow." Heath's brow went up. "She didn't respond to anybody like that before I left."

"Yeah, well, Daisy and I have gotten close since you two left," Barbie said, her tone sullen. "She's all I had left."

Heath's chest constricted with all-too familiar emotion. Daisy was all he had left too. All he had left of Davy. He watched as she charged toward them, then pulled up at the last minute, whinnying as Barbie jogged out to meet her. The two of them looked like naturals together.

"You wanna go for a ride, girl?" Barbie asked her. "Wanna show Heath what you can do now?"

Heath's smile dropped. "Don't push her too hard. She's not used to that."

Barbie glanced incredulously at him before nudging Daisy closer to the stable. "You've been gone. You don't know what she's used to. And for the hundredth time, Daisy isn't a fragile flower. Are you, girl?"

Daisy snorted, bobbing her head as they reached the stable door. Barbie marched inside to fetch her saddle and a blanket. Heath followed, searching for Buck, his trusty old gelding. If Barbie was going to push Daisy beyond her comfort zone, then he was going to be there to put a stop to it. Just like Davy would have wanted.

They worked side-by-side saddling their horses. Heath was out of practice, or so he told himself, so Barbie had Daisy fixed up and ready to go before he was done with Buck. He refused to admit that his bum leg had anything to do with his slowness, or with the wince that he couldn't hide as he pulled himself into the saddle.

"You okay?" Barbie asked as they started off to the gate that led into a smaller corral.

"I'm fine," Heath answered. "Just a little rusty."

She hummed, glancing pointedly at his leg, then dismounted to open the gate. Heath rode Buck through, then watched as Barbie brought Daisy through, shut and latched the gate, and mounted with swift, sure movements. They repeated the sequence at the other side of the corral.

"Okay, I get the point," he said with a smirk as she remounted for the second time.

"What point?" she asked, her smile entirely too innocent.

He shook his head, unsure whether he wanted to kiss her or call her out for showing off. "I get that you're strong and nimble while I'm recovering from a bullet in the thigh. I get that you know your way around the ranch, that you know what you're doing, boss lady."

Her easy look turned into a frown. "I'm not trying to show off. I'm just doing my job."

He wasn't sure he believed her. Not after everything she said about having to try to work twice as hard to prove she could do a man's job. "Go ahead, then," he said. "Do your job."

He smiled, but her frown only darkened. "I will. And there's something I want to show you."

"Okay, what?"

They'd walked their horses along the edge of the old barrel racing course that Kathleen had made their dad build years ago. It had been cleaned up a bit since he'd left for the war. The splintering barrels had been replaced by stacks of old car tires, and the course itself was well-maintained.

But that didn't prepare him for the sudden shout from Barbie, or the way Daisy jumped into action, flying toward the course. Heath's heart shot to his throat as Daisy headed for the first set of barrels. All he could think about was her bones breaking and the screams that would follow. His imagination mingled them with Davy's screams and shouts on the battlefield.

"Barbie, stop!" he shouted, but she didn't hear him.

Daisy made it around the first barrel and shot off toward the second. Heath stood in his stirrups, heart thundering against his ribs. She would fall. She would be thrown. Daisy would trip and it would all be over. He'd lose another friend. He'd lose Davy's horse. There'd be nothing he could do about it. Again. He'd be helpless and hopeless, and his world would fall apart. Again.

His thoughts spun out of control so hard that it seemed as though he blinked and Daisy was through the course, trotting toward him. Barbie sat, smiling and panting, in the saddle.

"See?" she said, glowing with exertion. "She loves it. She's dying to race."

"No." Heath gripped his reins hard to keep his hands from shaking. "Don't ever do that again." His voice came out rough and hollow.

"Why? It's what Daisy was born to do." Barbie's frown held more than frustration. She was studying him.

"She could have been hurt. You both could have been hurt."

"Come on. Give me more credit than that." Barbie's frown disappeared, replaced by a teasing look. She rode Daisy right up to Buck's side and reached out to grip his arm. "I know what I'm doing."

Part of Heath wanted to lean into her, wanted to pull her onto the saddle with him and hold her until his shaking stopped. The rest of him pulsed as though he were in a combat zone.

"I said no," he snapped, yanking Buck's reins to get away from her. "It's too dangerous."

"It's not dangerous it's—"

"Will you just listen to me," he shouted. "I'm trying to save your life."

Barbie's mouth snapped shut and her face flooded with color. She swallowed hard, then stared at him with far more emotion than he wanted to deal with. She knew. He'd slipped up, and she knew him well enough to know that his leg wasn't the only wound he'd brought home from Vietnam.

But where he expected cooing and coddling, all he got was a firm, wary look.

"I don't know anything about this sort of stuff, Heath," she said, her voice low and calm. "But I know you have to work through it. I'm not saying it'll be easy," she said as though she expected him to interrupt, "but you have to get back up on the horse." She paused, then added. "Just make sure you get back on your own horse and not mine."

Her eyes bored into him as she said it, and oddly enough, it came as a comfort to Heath. He had his battle scars, but Barbie was still at war. And maybe, just maybe, that meant she would understand. She might even understand some things he didn't.

He nodded. "Let's ride," he said, his voice hoarse.

She nodded in return, and her shoulders softened as she tapped Daisy into motion.

## 4

Over the next few days, Barbie couldn't shake the irritating sense that Heath needed her help in some way. On the one hand, it was obvious that his experience in Vietnam and losing Davy had scarred him. How could it not? But guessing the obvious and knowing what to do about it were two different things. Heath worked steadily in the stables, sometimes taking directions from her, sometimes doing his own thing. And though she was tempted to call him out for undermining her authority, the distracted, troubled look in his eyes when he brushed Daisy down, instead of parceling out the carrots and apples the Langley horses were supposed to be getting as a treat, kept her from saying anything.

By the day of Heath's welcome home party, he'd

developed a poker face that would have convinced anyone he had put the war and everything about it behind him. It would be more than enough to fool the legions of friends and well-wishers that were expected to descend on Legacy Ranch, but it didn't fool Barbie.

"You gonna be okay?" she asked as she passed Heath on the porch while heading in to give Maura a hand setting up.

"Yeah," Heath answered. "Why wouldn't I be?" He met her eyes, and Barbie saw steel resolve behind his easy smile. He was gearing up for a different kind of battle.

"If you need anything, just let me know," she told him with an arched eyebrow, then marched on into the house.

"Oh, Barbie, there you are." Maura caught her almost as soon as she was through the door. "I'm so glad you're here. I need your help bringing some old tablecloths and things down from the attic."

"Sure thing, Mrs. Langley."

Barbie followed Maura up the staircase, around a corner, then up a second, narrower staircase to the attic. There was something fun and mysterious about attics, especially in houses like the Langleys'. It had been there in one form or another since the mid-19th century, and it looked like it. The exposed rafters had a sense of age to them, a feeling that they carried the secrets of generations. Old photo albums and even older books shared the space with trunks that looked to be a hundred years old and stacks of records that she and Heath had listened to as kids.

Barbie stepped over to one of the shelves, picking up what looked like an ancient family Bible. No sooner had she lifted the front cover, than an old photo slipped out.

"Oh!" Cheeks burning with embarrassment, she leaned over to retrieve the photo. It was of Maura and Aidan, and it looked like a wedding picture. But neither of them looked particularly happy.

"Mrs. Langley, have you seen this?" she asked, showing the photo to Maura.

Maura frowned and pushed through a few old boxes of toys to take the photo. As soon as she saw it, she laughed. "That was quite a day."

"You and Mr. Langley don't look particularly happy," Barbie said.

Maura chuckled as she looked at the photo with a long, thoughtful look. "Neither of us was keen on getting married. Our parents set it up as a way to save the ranch."

"I didn't know that." Barbie wasn't sure whether she should dig into the story more or leave it alone.

Maura sighed, slipping the photo back into the Bible and handing it to Barbie. "Things worked out absolutely as they should have in the end. It's funny how life does that. And Aidan and I couldn't be happier now."

Barbie smiled. "I hope I have a love like that someday."

"You will," Maura grinned, patting her arm. "Maybe sooner than you think." She paused. "The old linens and things are over here," she said, climbing over a few boxes of Christmas decorations and old records to get to a tall wardrobe that looked as old as the house itself. "We only use them for special occasions."

She opened the wardrobe, and Barbie gasped. Next to the shelves of neat, folded linen were several vintage gowns. A few looked to be from the fifties, but a gown of delicate silk in a turn-of-the-century style hung right beside them, and a bodice of pale green muslin with delicate embroidery hung next to that. But the prize of the collection was a faded, though carefully preserved, wedding dress.

"Look at this," Barbie said, putting the old Bible aside and moving to reverently take the dress out of the wardrobe to look at it. "Wow. This must be ancient."

Maura laughed. "Parts of it are. The lace came all the way from Ireland when the very first Langleys came to this country in the 1850s."

"Really?" Barbie glanced to Maura, then returned to studying the dress. "I'm almost afraid to touch it."

"It's not as fragile as you think. I wish I'd had the chance to wear it on my wedding day."

Barbie's brow flew up. "You didn't?"

Maura laughed. "No. Like I said, mine and Aidan's wedding was a bit…rushed. Our parents sprung the whole thing on us with no time for us to prepare. Or back down."

"You aren't planning to have history repeat itself, are you?" Barbie laughed.

Maura smoothed a hand over the ancient wedding dress with a laugh and a fond sigh. "The thought might have crossed my mind," she said with a secret smile. "Anyhow, aside from me, it's been a tradition for all Langley brides to wear the dress, or at least the lace, which has been reworked a few times, on their wedding day." A knowing smile spread across her aged features. "Maybe someday soon you'll get to wear it."

An awkward, excited shiver shot down Barbie's spine. She hung the dress back in the wardrobe. "I don't know."

Maura grinned at her. "The way you and Heath have taken up together since he's been home? If that's not what I think it is, then I'm a monkey's uncle."

Barbie laughed, reaching for the stack of linens Maura took from the shelf and handed to her. "I'll admit that Heath and I are close. I'll admit that things started to heat up between us before he left for Vietnam." Her cheeks heated as she spoke. "But you know Heath came back with a lot more on his plate than he left with."

Maura's smile tensed. "I know." She looked away, a maternal sadness in her eyes as she fetched the rest of what she needed from the wardrobe. "No mother wants to see their son hurting. And none of us are fool enough to think that his experiences over there haven't changed him. Especially losing Davy the way he did."

Barbie's throat closed up her chest tightened at the mention of her old friend.

"That's why I think you're so good for him," Maura went on, stepping past Barbie and heading downstairs. "You two have a special connection, you always have. And you were Davy's friend too. I just hope...." She let her words fade as they stepped into the noisy hum of the house as everyone else rushed around getting ready for the party.

When they reached the first floor and headed back out to the porch and the tables that had been set up on the lawn, Barbie said, "I know, Mrs. Langley." She set her load of linens on one of the tables and peeked up at the porch, where Heath was talking to a newly-arrived guest, one of their friends from high school. "But give us time before you start writing our wedding vows."

"Of course, dear," Maura laughed.

"And remember, I have a job. I wouldn't want to drop that just to get married."

"You wouldn't?" Maura blinked. Then she shook her head and laughed. "I keep forgetting that young women these days have ambitions. Maybe it's because I'm so content with the way my life turned out." Her gaze drifted off across the lawn, landing on Aidan, who was busy firing up a huge grill along with Chip. She sighed, her face filling with love as she watched her husband.

Barbie couldn't help but smile, her heart feeling light. Love like the kind Aidan and Maura had didn't come along every day. She was convinced that things were simpler back in the day, that men and women knew where they stood and knew what they expected from each other. She peeked up at Heath again, wondering what he expected from her. Come to think of it, she wasn't sure what she wanted from him either. All she knew was that she wanted him to be happy and to feel whole.

He must have felt her watching him, because he turned from his conversation and met her eyes. The stress in his expression was obvious, but the moment Barbie sent him a reassuring smile, he relaxed. With a hint of a smile, he turned back to his conversation, and Barbie felt a rush of relief and purpose. She could help him get through all the things that had happened to him. It would all be okay if they stuck together.

That feeling of certainty and confidence stayed with Barbie as she helped Maura and Heath's sisters bring food out to the tables and greet their guests. It felt good to be considered part of the Langley family, even if it meant she had to endure more than a few questions about her and Heath, and about whether she would quit her job to be a homemaker if things turned out the way everyone expected them to. No one seemed to believe her when she insisted that her job came first. She was right on the verge of being irritated about people's insistence that she'd change her mind once she had a ring on her finger when a hush fell over the guests closest to the edge of the lawn, where cars were parked. Marge and Robert Sudgeon, Davy's parents, had arrived.

Barbie broke away from her conversation with a couple of school friends to meet them. "Mr. and Mrs. Sudgeon, it's so good to see you here." She gave Marge a hug, feeling her heart break in her chest as she did.

"Thanks, sweetie," Marge whispered.

Barbie took a step back and studied Marge to make sure she was really okay. She wore a perfect, crisp blue skirt suit, completely inappropriate for a barbecue, and her pillbox hat was perched just so on her head. The lines around her mouth and eyes were the only thing about her that weren't exactly in order, and she was far paler than anyone should have been in summer. Everyone in New Dawn Springs knew that she'd been coping with Davy's death by cleaning and organizing anything that came within ten feet of her. Robert wasn't much better, though he was dressed in slacks and a button-down shirt rather than church clothes. Overall, though, Barbie was surprised they'd come to the party. Davy was their only child, and if it had been her, the pain would have been too great.

More and more of the party guests hushed as the Sudgeons headed toward the porch. What was supposed to be a festive occasion suddenly felt more like a funeral. As soon as Heath glanced down from his porch conversation and saw Davy's parents coming, he froze. The color drained from his face. He handed off his beer to the guy next to him and strode to the stairs and down to the lawn to meet the Sudgeons.

Everyone was silent as Heath marched up to them. "Mr. and Mrs. Sudgeon," he said, then hesitated, his mouth open.

It was so quiet that Barbie could hear the wind, could hear the horses neighing down in the paddock. She could also hear her heart as it pounded in her chest. Her senses prickled the same way they did before Daisy burst into a run. She was determined to be ready in case...in case.... She didn't know in case of what.

"I'm sorry," Heath said at last, his voice cracking. "I did everything I could, but...."

"We know, son," Robert said, his voice thin and broken. "We know."

He stepped into Heath and hugged him like a

father, thumping him on the back. Barbie's throat closed tight, and tears stung in her eyes, but she was determined to be strong. Heath's face was a mask of conflicted emotions as he moved to hug Marge, who broke down into silent tears.

"Thank you," Marge whispered, hugging Heath tightly.

Barbie took a half-step back, feeling as though she'd trod on sacred ground. The moment should have been between Heath and Davy's parents alone, but instead, everyone who had come to the party was watching. Barbie searched for Maura, and when she found her, standing next to Aidan at the grill, she did her best to communicate with a look that something needed to be done to shift everyone's focus.

Fortunately, Aidan nodded, then took charge. He left the grill, marching to Heath and the Sudgeons. "Rob, Marge. We're so glad you could come. Do you want a burger?"

It was simple, silly, and unimportant, but the offer of food was exactly what the moment needed to keep it from getting out of hand. Robert accepted the offer enthusiastically, escorting Marge to the grill, everyone else's conversations picked up, and Heath breathed a sigh of relief as the focus shifted off him.

"Are you sure you're okay?" Barbie asked as he rubbed his hands over his face.

He sucked in a breath. "Yeah. I think so. Where's my beer."

In spite of the swirl of emotions in her chest, Barbie grinned. "Jake has it." She nodded to the porch, where the school friend Heath had been talking to raised the can.

"Thanks," Heath whispered, giving her a look that encompassed more than locating his beer. He hesitated, then nodded to Barbie and headed up to the porch.

Barbie let out a long, nervous breath, then headed to the table of food to make sure everything was where it should be. She hadn't realized her hands were shaking, but as the mood lightened and laughter filled the air again, she calmed down. Aidan and Maura were taking care of the Sudgeons, Heath had returned to his conversation on the porch, and the anxious moment had passed.

"I'm sure you had something to do with that, Davy," she murmured as she moved on to the drinks table and fetched a beer from the cooler for herself. She glanced up at the sky and winked. "Thanks."

As tensions eased, Barbie actually started to have a good time. She talked to a few of her friends from school, got into a silly conversation with her good friend Doris about the latest Beatles album, and gorged on chips and onion dip when Kelly brought them out. Things were going well after all.

She finally made her way over to Heath's side, braving the slew of comments she knew standing with him would raise.

"So, are you two finally gonna get together now that Heath's back?" Jake asked what three people had asked in the previous fifteen minutes.

Barbie glanced up at Heath with a look that could be considered an eye-roll. "Give the man a chance to settle in again before taking on his next project," she laughed.

"We'd all love to see it happen," Jake's girlfriend, Rita said with a wink.

"Yes, and I know Davy would love it." The conversation screeched to a halt as Marge joined them, Robert by her side.

"We always thought Barbie and Davy would get together," Robert said with a fond, sad smile. "But Davy constantly told us that it was you two, not him."

Heat splashed to Barbie's face so fast she leaned back against the porch rail to keep from falling over.

"Yeah, I'll admit that Davy knew more than most people," she said, adding an anxious laugh.

Heath managed to keep his composure, but his jaw flexed and his lips pinched as though he wanted to say something but couldn't. He reached out and rested a hand on the small of Barbie's back, but she knew good and well it wasn't a possessive gesture or a declaration of anything. He needed her support.

"We'll see what happens," she said, feigning casualness as she smiled up at Heath.

An awkward silence fell between them all. Jake and Rita looked as though they'd rather be somewhere else as they glanced between Heath and the Sudgeons. At last, Robert broke the silence.

"There's something we wanted to talk to the two of you about," Robert began.

"Oh?" Barbie stood straighter.

"Yes, Robert and I have been talking about it," Marge glanced to her husband. "You both know that Davy loved his horse, Daisy, more than just about anything in the world."

"Yes, of course," Barbie said, near tears all over again. She forced them down with a smile. "I've been doing my best to take good care of Daisy. She's thriving."

"Oh, believe us, we know," Robert said. "Davy would be proud of the way you've cared for her."

"Especially since he put so much effort into keeping her alive those first few weeks," Marge said, then swallowed.

They all knew. Daisy had had a difficult, breech birth, and things had been touch and go for the first two weeks. The vets had all said that without Davy's constant care, Daisy probably wouldn't have made it.

"That's why we've decided we'd like you to have her," Robert went on, his voice rough. "Both of you," he added.

Barbie glanced to Heath. "Both of us?"

"Yes," Marge pushed on, blinking fast and trying to smile. "We've talked about who would be the best owner for Daisy now that…"

"And in the end," Robert picked up as Marge wiped a tear from her face, "we decided that Davy would want both of you to own her jointly."

A wave of elation was quickly replaced by uncertainty in Barbie's chest. "Both of us."

"That's not going to be a problem, is it?" Marge recovered enough to ask. "I don't really know much about the legalities of owning a horse, but since Daisy is boarded here, it seemed natural."

"It's not a problem," Heath said. The fact that

he'd found his voice at last felt like a good sign to Barbie. "I don't know how to thank you."

"Neither do I," Barbie said. She stepped forward to hug Marge. "We'll take excellent care of Daisy."

"I know you will," Marge said, hugging her back. "And I...I was thinking that Heath could ride Daisy in the Fourth of July parade next week." Her eyes filled with hope as Barbie stepped back to Heath's side.

"Oh," Barbie said. "I was going to ride her and enter her in some of the races."

"Are you sure Daisy's up to racing?" Robert asked. "She was such a tender little filly."

"She's grown into a fine, strong mare." Barbie had to work to keep her smile in place. Davy's parents had just made an extraordinarily generous gesture. It would be wrong of her in every way to talk back to them or contradict their wishes, but that didn't stop frustration from bubbling up inside of her.

"I wish I could ride Daisy in the parade." Heath stepped in before Barbie could say something she'd regret. "Dad had his heart set on me riding Finn, though. Finn's a direct descendant of one of the first horses born on Legacy Ranch."

Barbie hadn't heard any such request from

Aidan, but whether Heath was telling the truth or whether he was making a gentle excuse so that Barbie could ride Daisy, she was grateful.

"Of course," Marge nodded, smiling and glancing from Heath to Barbie. "I understand completely, And I know Davy would be just as happy for you to ride Daisy, Barbie."

"It will be an honor." Barbie hugged her one more time. "And I hope you'll be able to come see Daisy race when—"

"We'll talk about that some other time," Heath cut in. "If you don't mind, the smell of those burgers has my stomach about ready to run down to the grill without me. Barbie, do you want to come get a burger?"

Before Barbie could say more than, "Sure," Heath grabbed her hand and crossed the porch to the stairs with her. As soon as they stepped from the path to the grass, Heath let out a breath.

"Sorry if that was awkward for you," she said, leaning closer.

"I'm fine," Heath insisted in the voice that let Barbie know he wasn't. Before they reached the line of people waiting for burgers or dogs at the grill, though, he steered her to the side and leaned in close. "We need to discuss this thing about Daisy racing."

"What, now?" Barbie blinked, but before Heath could take the conversation in a direction she didn't want to go, she said, "Daisy is strong, healthy, and desperate to race."

"Davy would kill us if she was hurt."

As soon as the words left Heath's lips, his face pinched with pain. Not only did the color leave his cheeks, for a moment, he looked like he'd be sick.

Barbie grabbed his hand. "Breathe. It's going to be okay. And we're not going to talk about this now."

Heath nodded and swallowed.

"We're at a party. Everyone is happy to see you. We're going to put up with everyone hinting that we should get married. We're going to get annoyed with them, but we're going to keep smiling. Everything else can wait."

"Okay." He drew in a long breath, then burst into a weak laugh, shaking his head. "Everyone *is* pestering us to get together, aren't they?"

"More than you know," she replied through clenched teeth.

He squeezed her hand, looking into her eyes. "It wouldn't be so bad, would it?"

For a moment, the Heath she'd started to fall in love with two years ago was back in his eyes. His humor and warmth was right there on the surface, bright and undamaged. It gave Barbie hope. Time. All they needed was time, and everything would work out.

"How about that burger now?" she said, letting his hand go and stepping sideways to get in line.

"Sounds like a great idea."

5

The Fourth of July had always been Heath's favorite holiday. Nothing beat a parade, a picnic, and fireworks. At least, nothing had beat those things before. The moment he reached the fairgrounds in New Dawn Springs, where the parade started and would end after looping through the main streets of town, he knew he was in for more than he'd bargained for.

"Welcome home, soldier." Old Mr. Grummond saluted him as Heath rode Finn toward the area where other riders were gathering. Barbie was already there on Daisy, laughing with one of her friends.

"Hey, Mr. Grummond." Heath nodded. "Beautiful day, isn't it?"

Mr. Grummond nodded, but launched straight into, "Where's your uniform, son?"

Heath glanced down at his plain clothes, then at Mr. Grummond's crisp World War Two uniform. The whole thing must have been over twenty-five years old, but it was in perfect condition, and the medals pinned to Mr. Grummond's chest sparkled.

"My uniform got mildewed," Heath lied. "It didn't do so well in the jungles over there." In truth, his uniform was in reasonable shape. He wasn't, though. Every time he even looked at his dress green jacket and the medals and pins affixed to the chest, all he could see were bloodstains and sweat.

Mr. Grummond smiled at him all the same. "Well, we'll be proud to have you march with us this morning, son."

"I'll be proud to be there with you, sir."

That much wasn't a lie. Heath nodded and nudged Finn on. He was proud of the service he rendered to his country. It was what he and Davy had dreamed about for ages. Serving wasn't the problem. Coming home alone was.

"Hey, Heath. What's this I hear about you and Barbie Rose?" The question came from Kenny Wallace, who had been in the class below Heath, Davy, and Barbie in school.

Heath twisted in his saddle, searching for Kenny. He found him standing with a cluster of other vets, wearing his uniform jacket the way Heath couldn't. One of Kenny's sleeves was pinned to his shoulder where his left arm should have been, but the smile on Kenny's face was indelible.

Still, Heath stared for too long before answering in a hollow voice, "Where did you hear that?"

Kenny shrugged. "It's all over the place. I always thought the two of you would end up together. Or if not you and her, then Barbie and Davy."

Cold fingers of dread spread through Heath's gut. He'd be hearing about Davy all day. The only way to deal with it was to buck up, take deep breaths, and face it all head-on.

He faked a grin. "Yeah, Barbie and I have been talking a lot since I got back." He dismounted, figuring it was rude to carry on a conversation from the top of a horse.

Kenny reached out with his whole arm and stroked Finn's back. "You lucky dog. Guys have been trying to catch Barbie's eye all year with no luck."

"Really?" Heath raised his brows.

"Sure," Kenny laughed. "She's sweet, she's cute, and she landed that job at your family's ranch. A girl like that could take care of a guy."

The comment didn't sit right. "She's a woman who can take care of herself too."

"Exactly." Kenny smiled, clearly missing the point.

Heath wasn't sure if he'd been missing the point too. Barbie was more than competent. She knew how to be in charge of things, even if guys like Rick gave her a hard time. It dawned on him that he should trust her a little more.

He glanced to the side, to where Barbie was still chattering away with her friends, but his eyes dropped to Daisy. He could trust Barbie on just about anything, but not with Daisy's life and well-being. He owed it to Davy to make sure his horse stayed healthy and whole, unlike—

He swallowed and turned back to Kenny. His old friend's smile felt completely at odds with the empty sleeve of his jacket. To his surprise, Kenny thumped his arm with his good hand.

"Hey," he said softly. "I get it, man. We all came back with wounds, but not all of them are visible."

"I didn't—"

Heath stopped himself before he could deny his wounds. Kenny deserved better than that. All of the vets milling around with them, waiting for the parade to start, deserved better. Kenny wasn't the only one with visible wounds. Sam Heldon walked with a cane now. Nathan Cavasos had a scar across his cheek. And Lenny Kowalski sat in a wheelchair, the stumps of his legs barely reaching past the seat. At the same time, they all seemed to be in a relatively upbeat mood.

Heath took a breath, then thumped Kenny's arm in return. "Yeah." It was all he could say, but it covered everything that needed to be said.

"You gonna march with us or are you riding with the rest of the horses?" Kenny asked.

Heath glanced from the group of vets his age to the old-timers from the Second World War, and one or two still kicking from the First. He looked beyond them to the horses and Barbie. She picked just that moment to look up at him and smile. It was as if the sun had come out from behind a cloud.

"I get it," Kenny said with a laugh. "You go and ride with your girl."

Heath turned back to him. "Nah, I belong here with you. She'll understand."

"What about your horse?"

"He can ride with me," Mr. Proust, a veteran of the Korean War who owned another ranch nearby, butted into their conversation. "Every army needs a cavalry, after all."

Heath and Mr. Proust weren't the only vets to ride in the end. One of the other local ranch owners who had fought in World War Two rode with them, along with a guy Heath vaguely knew from rodeo events who had done a tour in Vietnam a few years before him. The vets on foot and in wheelchairs walked ahead of them, and their entire group led the parade.

Heath had participated in the parade more than a few times—from riding his decorated bike with the rest of the little kids to marching with the Boy Scouts to playing the trumpet in the high school marching band—but leading the parade was a whole different beast. He did his best to smile and wave at the crowd that gathered to wave flags or salute them. The streets of New Dawn Springs were lined with smiling, proud faces. Kevin had flown in the night before, and it was a treat to see his big brother waving at him along with the rest of the family.

But all Heath could think about was Davy. Davy was the one who should ride at the front of the parade. Davy was the one who lapped up this kind of attention. He wouldn't have gloated in it, but he sure had loved representing his country.

By the time the parade looped all the way through town and returned to the fairgrounds,

Heath's smile had faded. In its place was an uneasiness and the need to get away from the past.

"How are you holding up?" Barbie asked, shaking him out of his gloom, as she rode up to him. The rest of the parade participants were dispersing, and the edge of formality had disappeared.

"I'm good." Heath shrugged, looking for anything else to talk about. "How's Daisy doing?" They stood close enough that he could lean over and pat Daisy's neck.

"She's fine," Barbie said. "Although crowds make her jumpy."

Tension splashed through Heath. "Then you should take her home right away. Don't upset her. Davy wouldn't like it."

Barbie's expression went blank, but Heath swore he could see frustration in the flash of her eyes. "Daisy's fine. What I meant was that she gets excited around crowds and wants to run, to show off."

Heath's mouth twitched into an awkward smile. "Kind of like Davy."

Barbie reached out and squeezed his arm. "I know how hard today is for you without him."

"It's not—" Heath blew out a breath through his nose, rubbing a hand over his face. He needed to stop with the knee-jerk need to deny people when they pointed out the obvious. But he hated feeling so breakable. He took in a breath and rolled his shoulders. "Are you sure Daisy isn't overtired or in danger of bolting and hurting herself."

"I'm absolutely sure of it," Barbie replied with a bright smile. "And I'll prove it to you."

"How?"

"Come on."

She winked, then nudged Daisy to walk. Heath didn't have much choice but to follow her. They wound their way through the growing crowds that were arriving at the fairgrounds as the parade finished. Most of the horses and riders were making their way to the far end of the field with them. Temporary stalls had been set up for anyone who wanted to park their horse and walk around for a while, but Barbie looked as though she were headed for the racetrack at the extreme end of the field.

"You're not thinking of racing Daisy, are you?" Heath asked.

"Of course I'm going to race her. And I'm going to win, too."

The look Barbie sent him over her shoulder sent a flash of heat through him. He suddenly wished that it were any other day, and that they were riding out alone in the field in back of Legacy Ranch. Riding, and then stopping and rolling around in the tall grass for a while.

He blinked as Barbie picked up her pace, joining the group of riders who were waiting to race. For that one second, the second after she looked at him, everything else had gone away. He was just a horny guy staring at a girl he liked. Moments like that made everything in the last two years' worth it.

"Where do I sign up for the race?" Barbie called over the conversations of the men sitting on horseback at the entrance to the racetrack.

Mr. Humphries leaned to the side and craned his neck to get a look at Barbie from his place next to the gate. "Ladies' race is at quarter to noon," he said.

"What about this race?" she asked.

Heath knew in an instant what would happen next. He nudged Finn closer to Barbie and Daisy.

"Men only in this race," Mr. Humphries said.

"Come on, Mr. Humphries." Barbie grinned at the older man, planting a hand playfully on her hip. There was steel in her eyes, though. "Daisy here could outrun this whole pack."

Mr. Humphries chuckled. Several of the other men did too. "Sorry, Barbie. I'm sure Daisy will do fine in the ladies' race."

"Why shouldn't we race with everyone else?" Barbie pressed on, her smile dropping.

More chuckles followed her question, but they were tense rather than jovial. Mr. Humphries glanced past Barbie to Heath. "You responsible for this little lady, Heath?" he asked.

Barbie's back was up in a second, even before Heath could answer, "Barbie's responsible for herself, Mr. Humphries. But if you all are too chicken to let her race with you...."

"Nice try," Mr. Humphries said with a teasing grin. "They teach you boys some mighty fine tricks in the Army, but that one ain't gonna work with me."

"Women have every right to race alongside men," Barbie said, denting the mood that everyone but her was trying to lighten.

"Barbie," Heath whispered, walking Finn close enough for him to touch her arm. She stiffened, but he went on with, "Take a walk with me."

She snapped her eyes to meet his. Her jaw was tense, and Heath felt an echo of the same quivering anticipation he'd felt every time he'd been asked to go out on patrol. Fortunately, she turned Daisy to walk away from the gate with him.

"It's not fair," she grumbled as soon as they were out of earshot of the other men.

"I know," he said, glancing back to the gate as Mr. Humphries opened it to let the men in. "Lots of things aren't fair."

"I'm sorry," Barbie sighed. "I wasn't thinking about it that way."

Heath glanced back to her. "Thinking about what?"

She leaned forward to rub Daisy's neck. "Lots of things aren't fair right now. Not just the way women are treated. It's not fair that you had to go fight someone else's war."

"I wasn't drafted, remember. I enlisted of my own free will."

"Yeah, but it still wasn't fair. And Davy didn't come back." Her shoulders dropped and she looked away from him.

It was an odd, new sensation. For months, even before he'd come home, people had tried to console him about Davy's loss. Suddenly, he was the one who needed to comfort Barbie about it.

"Why are we sitting around here moping?" he asked in a stronger voice. "Let's skip the races and go see if Betty Scofield made her homemade ice cream again this year."

Barbie cracked a smile. "She makes it every year."

"Then let's take these guys over to the stable for a couple hours and have some fun. Daisy looks like she could do with a rest anyhow." He nodded to Davy's horse—their horse.

Barbie arched her brow. "Daisy is disappointed not to get a chance to compete. She's dying to be a champion, you know."

"And I'm dying for an ice cream cone."

He didn't think his words were particularly challenging, but Barbie narrowed her eyes and stared at him all the same. A moment later, she gave up with a sigh and nodded.

"All right," she said. "You win this time. But we still need to talk about entering this tough old girl in the barrel races at the rodeo in two weeks."

Heath pushed aside the coil of worry that gripped him at the suggestion. It was more important for him to smile and stand by Barbie for the moment. But she was right, they did need to talk about Daisy's future.

As soon as Daisy and Finn were settled in the fairgrounds' stable, Heath took Barbie's hand and walked with her around the edge of the racecourse to the booths of food and games.

"Oh, now everyone's going to think we're a

couple," Barbie said, raising her hand in his for a moment.

"What, can't two good friends hold hands while walking around a Fourth of July celebration?"

She sent him a look that said he was an idiot. "Things haven't changed *that* much since you left."

He laughed. It felt easy and natural. "Well, what if we were a couple?"

"No." She shook her head, but she couldn't hide her grin or the mirth in her eyes.

"What do you mean, no?"

"I mean, no, you are not having this conversation with me and asking me to go steady in the middle of a crowded fairgrounds."

They passed a booth selling flossy, pink cotton candy, which was surrounded by giddy, bouncing children.

"Yeah, that's more of the kind of conversation we should have in the back of a car after dark," he joked. "Although I'm not sure how I'd fit in the back of that pokey old Beetle of yours."

Barbie laughed, her face going red. "I'm not doing it in the back of my car."

A couple of their classmates who had married right out of school and had two squirmy toddlers waved to them from the starting line of a race for babies who had only just learned how to walk a dozen yards away, and Heath waved back.

"So you are planning to do it with me then," he said as casually as if he were asking if she were planning to have blueberry pie for dessert at the picnic later.

"Heath, stop," she laughed, smacking his arm. "When did this conversation get so out of bounds?"

He shrugged, enjoying the way she flushed as he teased her. Heck, he enjoyed just walking through the throngs of celebrating people with her, feeling almost like life was as it should be. In fact, the only fly in the ointment was that Davy wasn't there.

"Do you want to do the egg toss?" Barbie asked once they'd made their way around all the booths. She nodded to the far end of the grounds where pairs were already lining up for the Fourth of July tradition

A wide grin split Heath's face. "Absolutely."

Barbie picked up her pace, dragging him with her. "Remember the summer we won?"

"Eight grade," he laughed. "Davy and Ben got out way, way early because Davy decided it would be more fun to throw the egg at Ben rather than letting him catch it."

Barbie laughed. "Do you remember how mad

Ben's mom got when he showed up at their picnic blanket with egg smeared all over his shirt?"

"'I just bought that shirt'." Heath imitated Ben's mom's tirade. "'I can't buy you anything nice anymore'."

"I felt so sorry for him," Barbie said with a snort as they reached the cartons of eggs for participants to use. She scanned them, then picked one.

"I felt sorry for Davy too," Heath chuckled, shaking his head. "Ben's mom told his mom, and Mrs. Sudgeon had Davy doing laundry for a month afterwards."

"And it wasn't even Ben's laundry." Barbie finished the story with a laugh.

They strode out to the end of the line, taking their places across from each other and waiting for anyone else who wanted to join in to line up with them. Heath glanced across at Barbie's grinning face, his heart beating loudly in his chest.

"You know, that might be the first time I thought about Davy without...." He let his sentence trail off as memories of shouting, gunfire, and the distinct smell of blood and the jungle washed over him.

"One step at a time, right?" Barbie asked, still grinning.

She brought him back before he could drift too far away. "Exactly."

It was a narrow escape, but he managed to keep his focus on the moment, on having fun. The egg toss began, and for the first few rounds, he and Barbie threw their egg back and forth across the growing distance with ease.

"It's all coming back to me now," Heath called across to her once they were about ten yards apart. He tossed the egg.

Barbie caught it with relative ease. "Really?"

"Yep. We're gonna win this thing."

"You think?" she asked. As soon as the word was given, she wound up and pitched the egg at him with full force.

It hit him square in the chest, breaking with a splat. Yellowy yolk spread across his shirt, and she burst into laughter.

For a split-second, Heath thought he'd been hit. The dampness seeping through his shirt felt like blood. Fear shot through him. The whole world seemed to slow down.

But no, he was home. It was egg, not blood. Barbie was teasing him, reminding him of a time when things were good. She was trying to help.

He forced himself to smile, and the world sped

up again. Barbie was stumbling toward him, one hand to her mouth, laughing up a storm. That was all he needed. His smile turned genuine, and he rushed to meet her, arms outstretched. He grabbed her in a bear-hug, smearing the egg from his chest across her. She squealed and yelped as he lifted her off her feet.

"Just what do the two of you think you're doing?" an angry, woman's voice cut into their moment of merriment from the side.

Heath put Barbie down, grabbed her hand, and stepped to the side, where Mrs. Wallace, Kenny's mom, was glaring at them.

"Sorry, Mrs. Wallace," Heath said, getting out of the way of the continuing egg toss. "We were just fooling around."

Mrs. Wallace continued to glare at them. "Where's your sense of dignity? You're a veteran, you have an image to uphold."

"We were just having fun, Mrs. Wallace," Barbie said, though her face had gone as pink as ever.

Mrs. Wallace wasn't appeased. She stepped closer to Heath, her voice shaking as she said, "My Kenny didn't go off to fight the communists, losing his arm, so that men like you could *joke around*."

"Honestly, ma'am," Heath said, at a loss of how

to appease her when she was obviously shaken. "We were just letting off some steam."

"You have a reputation to uphold," Mrs. Wallace insisted. "Times are hard enough without men like you taking your good fortune for granted. Look at Davy Sudgeon. He didn't come back at all. He—"

"We know, Mrs. Wallace," Barbie cut the woman off as Heath's insides froze. "He was our friend. Now, if you'll excuse us, we need to clean up."

Barbie tugged on Heath's hand, leading him away from Mrs. Wallace and the rest of the games. As much as Heath wanted to say something to make things right, he felt as though he were more likely to rail against Kenny's mom, to ask if she had any idea what he'd gone through trying to save Davy, all for naught. It was a blessing that Barbie pulled him away when she did.

"Let's walk around a little, shake that woman off," Barbie suggested.

"Yeah." Heath forced himself to breathe.

They walked back through the booths of food and smaller games, but Heath had a harder time soaking in the festive atmosphere. It was still the middle of the afternoon, but when a group of boys huddled behind one of the booths, looking like they were up to no good, set off a string of firecrackers in a metal bowl, Heath jumped and flinched. His heart shot into his throat, and it was all he could do not to run, to find cover. He didn't realize that he'd raised his arms to shield his head until the boys started shouting, "Sorry, sorry mister!"

"Show some respect," Barbie yelled at them, picking up her pace and dragging Heath away.

By the time they reached the stables at the other end of the grounds, Heath's nerves were shot and his stomach was in knots.

"Would you mind if I just took Finn and headed home?" he asked, hating the idea of giving up, but done with the whole day.

"I'll get Daisy and come with you," she said with a weary sigh. "I'm kind of done with this place myself."

"You don't have to leave if you don't want to."

She huffed a laughed and rolled her eyes as they entered the stable. "Believe me. I'm done. Besides," she said, a mischievous look coming into her eyes. "I just had an idea of something much more fun that we could do."

6

The holiday wasn't turning out the way Barbie hoped it would. She hated being turned away from a stupid race. It wouldn't have bothered her if it hadn't been such a sign of the times. But spending time with Heath was a perfect consolation prize. Even if tension rippled off him.

"I hate to keep asking, but are you sure you're okay?" she asked as they settled Daisy and Finn in the stable at Legacy Ranch.

Heath let out a long breath as he shut Finn's stall door and wandered over to where Barbie was finishing brushing Daisy. "Every part of me wants to tell everyone that I'm fine. I should be fine. I want to be fine."

"But you're not." Barbie glanced over her shoulder at him.

He'd crossed his arms and leaned against the side of the stall. A deep frown creased his face as he stared at a spot on the floor. "It's impossible to explain to people who've never been to war all the ways it changes you."

"I'm sure," Barbie said, keeping her tone low and respectful. "Especially with Davy."

He nodded slowly, still staring at the floor. "I was with him, you know. When he died."

Barbie tossed the currying brush aside and faced Heath. "Yeah, you mentioned."

Silence followed. Barbie stroked Daisy's back a few times before heading out of the stall.

"Do you want to talk about it?" she asked Heath as she shut the door.

"No, I don't want to talk about it." He blew out a breath and raked a hand through his hair. "I don't ever want to talk about it. I don't want to remember it, and I don't want it to have happened." He paused. "But it's all been sitting there, festering inside me and I think...I feel like...." He made a frustrated noise.

"Like you should tell somebody."

"Yeah."

He looked at her in a way that sent a shiver down Barbie's spine. That kind of pain and horror was unimaginable to her. But Davy had been her friend, Heath was more than her friend, and for the love of both of them, she was willing to listen.

"Come on." She took his hand and started out of the stable. The ranch was quiet and peaceful with everyone in town celebrating the Fourth. Some of the Langley horses were out in the paddock, and the family dogs, Charlie and Mo, were lounging in the sun on the driveway, but those were the only signs of life.

All the same, instead of heading up to the house to sit on the porch, Barbie led Heath out along the carefully mowed paths through the meadow. The hot, July sun beat down on tall grass that waved in the slight breeze, smelling like summer should. Wildflowers dotted the green, and birds fluttered over it all, flitting from tree to tree around the edges of the meadow.

"All I know about Davy," Barbie began, "is that the two of you were on a patrol and got caught in an ambush. That's all his parents told us."

They stepped off the mowed path and headed through the grass to a large, shady tree.

Heath nodded. "We were lucky that night, I guess. In a way. Our commanding officer knew we were friends, but we didn't always get sent out together."

Barbie stayed silent, holding his hand and watching Heath carefully. He was already slipping off into his memories, so as soon as they reached the tree, she motioned for him to sit in the soft grass at the tree's base.

"You've got to understand what it was like out there in the swamp," he went on. It was the rainy season, and everything blurred together. The swamp grass was up to our asses, and the bugs were just terrible. But they were nothing compared to the human dangers." He rubbed a hand over his face and glanced to her. "The VC are masters of camouflage. They could hide behind a single blade of grass in the middle of the desert. We never knew how many were out there, and we never saw them coming."

His voice took on a hollow tone, and he glanced out over the tall grass. The whole world seemed to hold still to listen to his story.

"The crazy thing is, there wasn't anything unusual about that night. There was no big sign in the air, no feeling like anything was going to happen. It was just an ordinary night on patrol. You didn't talk if you knew what was good for you on those things, but Davy and I were relaxed. It was like any other night in high school when we used to sneak out here with a six-pack. I was about three seconds away from making some kind of joke."

He paused. Barbie could feel what would come next. Heath lowered his head, his eyes wide, but the look in them empty. She inched closer, slipping her arm around his back to rub it.

"The bullet came out of nowhere," he whispered at last. "Like a giant mosquito. It whizzed right past me and smacked Davy in the neck. And that was it."

Barbie's chest squeezed and her throat closed up. "That was it?" she asked, her voice a squeak.

Heath shrugged, tilting his head back and blinking at the sky. "I mean, pandemonium erupted after that. We'd walked into an ambush, but the guys weren't just going to take it. We fired back, and from what I've been told, we gave as good as we got and then some. But from the first second, all I could think about was Davy."

He lowered his head, and Barbie rested her chin on his shoulder.

"I fired a few shots, then turned to catch him when he fell," Heath went on. "I think we both knew that he was a gonner. He clutched at his throat, but there was blood everywhere. The bullet must have hit his jugular. He couldn't breathe, couldn't—" He stopped, swallowing convulsively, his ragged breath turning into a sob.

"It's okay," Barbie whispered. "You don't have to go on. I get it."

Heath sucked in a few more difficult breaths. It didn't take a genius to see how overcome he was. All Barbie could do was hug him and cry along with him.

At last, Heath recovered enough to say, "I kept firing, but I knew I had to get him out of there too. There wasn't an easy way to pick him up, but I tried, then I fired, then I tried some more. Then I got hit in the leg. That didn't stop me, though. I didn't even realize how bad my injury was until I'd carried Davy all the way out of the fight and emptied my gun. The fight was over in minutes anyhow. I collapsed, holding Davy in my arms."

As much as she wanted to say just the right thing to take Heath's pain away, she was beyond words. All she could do was hold him, resting her forehead against his shoulder.

"I wish Davy had had some great last words or something," he continued after a long pause. "I wish I'd been able to say goodbye or sorry, or that I could have taken a message back to his folks. But he was gone before I made it to safety. He...he must have died before I made it to safety myself. After that, I...." He stopped, swallowing hard.

Silence fell. It didn't matter how hard Barbie hugged him or how patiently she waited, whatever emotional battles Heath had gone through in that horrible moment, with Davy in his arms, were his and his alone. He closed his eyes, holding a hand to his face, his body rock-hard with tension.

It was a long time before he said, "I don't remember much for a few days after that. Bits and pieces, that's all. Then I woke up in a hospital near Saigon and started down the road to recovery." He shrugged, and his tension lessened. "And here I am now."

"You've come a long way." Barbie shifted so that she could throw both arms around him. "I'm so proud of you."

"Proud of me?" He huffed, shaking his head. "I didn't do anything to be proud of."

"Yes, you did," she insisted. "You fought for your country, and you did everything you could to save Davy."

"But I didn't."

"And that's not your fault." She paused. "You do know it's not your fault he died. It was war. Someone was a good marksman."

"I know." Heath let out a breath, his shoulders sagging. He glanced across the meadow. "I know on a rational level, but it's impossible not to feel like it's my fault all the same."

"Yeah." It was a stupid thing to say, but Barbie couldn't think of anything better. She couldn't think of anything that would take Heath's pain away, make him feel whole and happy again. Except....

She leaned in, resting her hand on the side of his face and turning it to look at her. She darted a glance at his lips before surging into him and kissing him. Heath flinched in surprise, but within seconds, the tension began to drain from his muscles as he kissed her back. He twisted to her, gathering her in his arms, and she passed control of their kiss over to him. Within no time, he was cradling her, his tongue teasing her lips in a bid to coax her to open for him. She had no problem doing just that. As their tongues touched, her heart seemed to grow in her chest.

"Wow," Heath said as they paused for breath. "That is not what I expected to happen."

"It's what was meant to happen," she answered, breathless. She stroked the side of his face, staring into his eyes. The haunted look of loss was still there, but it was tempered by the fierceness of the love she'd always known he had for her. "I want you to be happy, Heath," she said. "I always have. I love you, and it tears me apart to see you suffering."

He drew in a breath at the word love, something deep and heated flashing through his eyes. "I love you too," he said. "I just...I just worried that you wouldn't forgive me for not bringing Davy home."

"There's nothing to forgive," she said, threading her fingers through his hair, her gaze dropping to his lips. "The war was not your fault. You did everything you could. And I want to do everything I can to make things better for you."

She surged toward him again, slanting her mouth over his. It was a bold move, far more forward than good girls were supposed to be, but it felt right. Heath responded with enthusiasm, circling his arms tighter around her, his hands stoking her back. Their kiss grew hotter and hotter, and Barbie found herself wanting more and more from him, for him.

"Barbie, I don't know what I'd do without you," he said, his breathing ragged. He cradled the side of her face and looked into her eyes with a combination of temptation and torment. "I love you, I always have."

"I know," she said with a grin, then leaned in to kiss him again. She lowered her hand to his chest to find his heart beating like mad. Then she lowered it farther to tug his shirt out of his jeans.

As soon as her hand brushed across the bare skin of his side, he growled into their kiss and pulled at her shirt too. A shiver passed down her spine as he slid a hand up her side to cup her breast over her bra.

"We probably shouldn't do this," he whispered, even as his other hand slipped under her shirt and up her back to find the clasp of her bra. "We really shouldn't do this."

"Why not?" she said, then gasped as her bra came loose. He drew his hands forward to hold and squeeze her breasts. The shivers of pleasure she felt grew to the size of lightning bolts as she arched into his hands. Her breasts felt full and sensitive, and his touch sent sparks of heat straight to her core.

"I'm not that kind of guy," Heath went on, nibbling at her lips. "And you're not that kind of girl."

"I am when I'm with you," she whispered. She'd never wanted to break all the rules and be bad more in her life. It wasn't just because the sensations zipping through her were magical either. For the first time since coming home, Heath moved with ease. He'd dredged up so much by telling her about Davy, and now it was like he'd let it all go. She needed to help him finish that process, help him feel alive and like a man again.

Her hands shook slightly as she reached for the button on his jeans, but she needed to show him how much she wanted him right then. Her hands brushed against the bulge of his erection, and her pulse sped up.

"Barbie," he gasped as she tugged his zipper down and rubbed her hand over his rigid length. "Are you sure?"

"I've never been more sure of anything in my life. I want you, Heath."

He hummed and slanted his lips over hers, kissing her hard enough to coax a moan from her. She drew her hands up from his jeans to work the buttons of his shirt open, but she barely had time to undo more than a few before he moved, rolling to the side and easing her to her back in the grass.

His kiss grew more fervent as he started on the buttons of her shirt, continuing on to her jeans when they were all undone. Everything seemed to speed up and blur as they wriggled out of their clothes, tossing everything aside. Gooseflesh broke out on her skin as it was exposed to the balmy, July air, but the sight of Heath's body—his chest and arms first, then his powerful legs and his thick, firm erection—captivated her. She wanted to look at him, touch him, all of him.

He stared down at her, studying her body as she drank in the sight of him. "You're so beautiful," he said, a growl in his voice.

She could practically feel his eyes rake her, taking in her breasts and her parted legs. Being so exposed to him should have felt awkward, embarrassing, but it wasn't. She wanted him to see her that way, to see her as every bit as sexy as the centerfolds in men's magazines. There was a raw power in being seen that way, knowing that his penis stood tall and eager because of her.

"Kiss me," she said, reaching for him.

He let out a breath and slid his body over hers, covering her, their skin sliding together everywhere. It was the most wonderful sensation she'd ever felt. She raked her fingers across his bare back as their mouths met and claimed each other, dug her nails into his flesh as he reached for her breasts. She didn't have the experience to know what she was doing, and he didn't seem to be the expert lover that films always made romantic men out to be, but they were discovering love together, and that was all that mattered.

He left her lips to kiss his way down her neck

and across her collarbone and chest to her breasts. She sighed in encouragement as he cupped one and squeezed it, lifting it so that he could close his mouth over her nipple. A wordless cry of approval escaped from her as he tasted and suckled her. She ground her hips against his, her body needing to be one with his in ways she didn't entirely understand. His erection was hot and tempting between them, and she couldn't help but arch into it.

"Barbie," he gasped, his hands moving down her body. "I don't think I'm going to last long."

"I don't want you to," she said, kissing his lips lightly. "I want you inside of me."

"But I want you to enjoy this too."

"I will," she promised him.

A spark of mischief came over her, and she took his hand, leading it down. Good girl or not, she knew how to pleasure herself. Biting her lip, she locked eyes with Heath and guided his fingers to exactly the right spot. Slowly, she showed him just how to touch her to send intense pleasure spiraling through her.

"Like this?" he asked, catching on and circling her clit with a gentle touch.

She moved her hand away, letting him discover what he could do. "Yes," she panted. "God, yes."

The pleasure built quickly as he touched her,

and she let out increasingly urgent sounds. His body tensed, and the heat pouring off him turned more intense. He had a look of revelation in his eyes, as if the mysteries of the female body had just opened up to him. His gaze dropped from her eyes to her body as he continued to pleasure her, bringing her closer and closer to orgasm, but she didn't mind. In fact, she loved the feel of him watching her lose herself to pleasure, and when she couldn't hold on anymore, the orgasm that washed over her was stronger than any she'd ever experienced.

Whether Heath felt it or simply knew on instinct that it was time, he shifted over her, spreading her legs farther apart, and guided himself to her still throbbing entrance. He pushed inside with a groan of pleasure. The momentary flash of pain that accompanied his thrust was nothing, and as soon as he started moving inside of her, everything within Barbie began to coil and sparkle again.

He felt so perfect inside of her. The way he filled and stretched her was new and wonderful, but somehow as familiar as time itself. She clasped her arms and legs around him as his thrusts grew less controlled, more primal. The sounds he made as he mated with her were almost as good as the physical sensations, and within moments, her body was shuddering in orgasm again.

He cried out along with her, and she felt him tense, then relax in the most deliciously satisfying way. His thrusts slowed, and with a low, rumbling moan, he collapsed on top of her. His weight above her was delicious, as was the feeling that her body had finally been used for the purpose it was meant to fulfill. She'd never felt such wonderful pleasure, and knowing she'd given it in return was amazing.

After a moment, Heath recovered enough to roll to his side, drawing her against him in an embrace. "I'm not sure we should have done that," he whispered, kissing her lightly.

"Of course we should have. It was inevitable."

"It was wonderful."

She smiled and hummed, then kissed him. "Let's stay naked in the grass and be like those free-love hippies."

"I suddenly think they have the right idea," Heath laughed. "We'll grow our hair long, paint your Beetle with flowers and peace signs, and drive down to California."

"I think the horses might have a problem with that," she giggled.

"All right." He kissed her. She could feel him

against her thigh, growing hard again already. "We'll stay here."

"I like the sound of that," she sighed, arching into him and hoping he took the hint that she was more than ready to go again. "We'll stay right here together."

7

Throughout his time in Vietnam, Heath had managed to avoid the pitfall of readily available, cheap sex that had snagged so many of his buddies. But Barbie wasn't a desperate local girl on the verge of starvation. She was the woman he loved, had always loved. It had felt right and natural to make love to her under the spreading oak tree on the Fourth of July. Their families had asked where they'd gone the next day, why they hadn't shown up for the picnic or the fireworks. Heath had been able to make an excuse about the crowds being too much for him and the fireworks triggering bad memories—which was true—but for the first time since coming home, the war hadn't been at the front of his mind.

"Has Lady Bird had her medicine yet today?" he

asked with far more of a smile than the question warranted a week or so after things with Barbie heated up. She sat at her desk in the stable, her brow knit in thought, and he'd popped in just to see her before getting to work for the day.

"Yeah, why?" She glanced up, and a bright smile painted her face pink.

"She seems a little listless." It was ridiculous to discuss an aging horse with a grin on his face and a rush of blood to his nether-regions. Any excuse to talk to Barbie was one he would take, though.

Barbie hummed, tossed her pen down, and stood. "Let me come take a look at her."

She made it as far as the doorway where Heath stood before pausing. The two of them were a breath away. She glanced up at him, her mouth soft and her eyes inviting. It took every ounce of will-power Heath had not to slide his arms around her, press her body to his, and kiss her. It hadn't just been the Fourth of July. Twice since then, they'd snuck off to have sex, once in his truck and once at her house when her parents were out for the night. He'd been worried that what they were doing was foolish, until she'd surprised him by announcing she was on the pill. It was amazing how one little admission could make him understand how great the so-called Sexual Revolution was in an instant.

Although he fully intended to marry her. As soon as possible.

With one eyebrow arched, she slipped past him, walking down the row between stalls. Heath took a moment to watch her, admiring her backside, before following.

"What are you looking at?" she asked, a glint in her eyes, as she turned the corner to the row where Lady Bird's stall was.

"My future," Heath answered with a wink.

Barbie blushed and giggled, then shook her head.

"It's about time you got to work on her," Rick said, standing from the stall he'd been mucking out.

Heath winced. If he'd known Rick was within earshot, he wouldn't have flirted. "We're just having fun." He tried to shrug the whole thing off.

"Have all the fun you want," Rick said, thumping Heath's back as he passed. "I can't wait until you're the one in charge instead of her."

"I heard that, Rick," Barbie called from around the corner, even though she was out of sight. "And I'm not going anywhere."

Rick snorted and muttered, "Yeah right. I'm

counting on you, man." He thumped Heath's back again. "Babes these days have all gone crazy."

"Zip it, Rick." Heath narrowed his eyes and shook his head, hoping Rick would get the point, then marched on, catching up with Barbie. "Sorry," he said as he entered Lady Bird's stall.

Barbie shrugged, her attention already on the horse. "Why? You're not the jerk, he is."

"Yeah, well."

He couldn't think of anything else to say, so he stepped up to Barbie's side and watched her examine Lady Bird. It was clear from the way she smoothed her hands over the old nag's flanks and checked her legs that she knew what she was doing. Barbie had majored in equine science, after all. Most girls taking those courses went on to become veterinarians, but in typical Barbie style, she'd used her degree for something else. It was clear she was on top of things, though.

"I can't wait to see how you are with our kids," he said, leaning against the side of the stall.

She sent him a teasing glance. "Who said we're going to have kids?"

He chuckled. "I know, I know, we haven't discussed anything serious yet. But that discussion is coming."

Her grin widened. "Is it?"

"Someday." He pretended to be nonchalant when every fiber of his being wanted to get down on one knee and propose to her right then and there.

"What if I don't want to have kids," she said with a casual shrug, moving to check Lady Bird's head and teeth.

"Of course you want to have kids. All women want a family."

Her smile slipped. "Not all women." She glanced over, meeting his eyes. "What if I'm one of the ones who don't? You know we can control that kind of thing these days."

Prickles of warning shot down his back. "Yeah, but you do want kids, right?"

She stared at him for several long, painful seconds, her lips pursed. "Yeah, I do," she admitted at last. "But I'm not giving up my job just to have a family."

Heath's prickles turned into something deeper, like snakes in his gut. "Don't kids take a lot of time and attention?"

"Sure they do." She shrugged, but much of the humor had gone out of her expression. "So do horses. And I spent a lot of time and money learning how to care for them."

"Okay." Heath nodded slowly. "We don't have to worry about anything like this right now. Maybe you'll change your mind after we're married." He raised his eyebrows, waiting for her reaction to his assumption that a proposal was imminent.

To his surprise, she huffed out an impatient breath and stepped away from Lady Bird to scowl at him. "I'm not going to change my mind. Not now, not with a ring on my finger."

"Uh, oh." Heath frowned. "I wasn't trying to pick a fight."

Barbie let out a breath and rubbed her forehead. "I know you weren't. I just want to make sure you're clear about what I want and don't want from life." She paused, and when he didn't speak, she said, "I want this job. I want a family. I want you."

"In that order?" he asked, crossing his arms.

She dropped her head a fraction, biting her lip. "I don't know. Up until the other day, I didn't know 'us' was going to happen. I suppose I'll have to think about it."

He wasn't sure why, but her answer gave him the feeling that someone was playing tug-o-rope with his insides. On the one hand, he loved Barbie and wanted to support her, no matter what she did. On the other, women were supposed to stay home, once they married and had kids. Like his mom had. Her mom too. And Davy's mom. Heck, like every mom he'd ever known. Wasn't that what women wanted to do?

She shook herself out of her thoughts and marched past him into the aisle. "Lady Bird seems all right to me, but I think I'll have Dr. Jessup come take a look at her next week, just to be sure. In the meantime, I'm gonna saddle Daisy up and let her practice with the barrels."

Heath was so distracted by his confused thoughts that it took him a second to catch up to what she said. "Wait, you're gonna do what?" He followed her around the corner to where Daisy was munching on hay in her stall.

"Daisy and I are going to practice," she said. "The race is next week, after all."

"I thought we agreed that Daisy wasn't up to racing."

She stopped and spun around to face him. "Agreed? Heath, we didn't even talk about it."

"Maybe we should talk about it now."

She crossed her arms. "By 'talk about it' do you mean you telling me I can't race her the way she wants to race because she's a fragile flower?"

A burst of self-consciousness flooded Heath's

gut. Mostly because she'd hit the nail on the head. "I just don't think Davy would want you putting a horse he loved so much at risk."

She sighed and shook her head before marching into the stall. "Here we go again. I've been working with Daisy for two years now. She's so much more than you're making her out to be."

"But she'd always—"

"And if you can't trust me to know what I'm talking about, then we have a problem."

Heath's thought stopped like a record scratching. "You think I don't trust you?"

"Not the way you're acting about Daisy." She took a step closer to her.

He closed the distance between her. "I've trusted you with more than I could ever trust anybody else," he said in a low voice. "How can you throw that back in my face?"

"The same way you can ignore the last two years of my life and the work I've done here," she countered immediately.

Heath clenched his jaw and tried not to let the swirling mass of confusion that Barbie's attitude caused and the feeling that he didn't know where he was or what he was doing, even though he was home, drag him into anger. He took a deep breath.

"Look, I know that you know more about Daisy than I do. But please understand that I'm just looking out for her best interest. It's what Davy would have wanted."

"I do understand," she said, pressing a hand to her temples and squeezing her eyes shut. "That's why it's so hard."

"What do you mean?"

She opened her eyes and stared at him. "I understand that because you feel responsible for Davy's death—even though it wasn't your fault—you feel like you need to coddle Daisy. I understand that if she gets hurt, it's like Davy getting hurt."

"That's not—"

"But I'm telling you, this horse is a champion." She threw her arm out to where Daisy was watching them argue with large, baleful eyes. "I'm telling you that if you give her a chance to prove herself to you, she will. But you're not even willing to give her that."

He crossed his arms. "You're also telling me that Daisy isn't the only one who wants to prove herself. You're telling me that you're a champion too, and that you deserve a chance to do a man's job."

"A job is a job," she said, not denying him, but not agreeing either. "It should belong to the person who does it best, regardless of whether that's a man or a woman."

"I agree with you." He let his arms drop.

"Then why are you trying to push me out of my job?"

He shook his head. "I'm not trying to push you out of anything."

"No?" She arched a brow. "Then what's all that about quitting this job to raise kids when and if we have them?"

"He's doing what any man worth his salt should do," Rick chimed in from across the aisle of stalls.

Fury lashed through Heath, and he turned to glare at Rick. But a good portion of his frustration was with himself—for not remembering Rick was there, for not understanding what Barbie had to put up with, and for her not being willing to come down off her high horse to consider what he was saying. And behind the fury lurked a mountain of complete and utter bewilderment. Life was supposed to be simple, wasn't it? Love was supposed to be easy.

"Mind your own business, Rick," he snapped, figuring he could start breaching whatever the divide between him and Barbie really was by standing up for her.

"Only if you mind yours, boss," Rick growled back, then stomped out of the stable.

"See?" Barbie exclaimed as soon as he was gone. "I have enough trouble putting up with Rick without having to deal with it from you. So why won't you just believe me when I say that Daisy wants to race?"

"How did we get from flirting to arguing in ten minutes?" he asked instead.

"Maybe we jumped into things too fast," she replied, shaking her head and turning back to Daisy to lead her out of the stall and over to where the saddles were kept.

"Too fast," he repeated, shaking his head and running a hand through his hair. "Barbie, the two of us have been a lifetime in the making. The only thing that was too fast about the other day was how soon it was over."

Her cheeks flushed, and she sent him a sidelong look. She didn't have anything to add, though, no matter how long Heath waited to hear something. He watched her as she went about saddling Daisy. The war had left its scars on him, but in that moment, it was peacetime and returning home that hurt even more. He knew exactly how he wanted things to be, but had no idea how to get them there.

"Could you do me a favor and at least acknowledge that my heart is in the right place?" he asked once Daisy was saddled and Barbie led her out into the paddock to mount.

She lifted a boot to the stirrup and prepared to pull herself up, but paused and let out a breath. She hesitated, then glanced his way. "Can you acknowledge that I feel this horse speak to me, and what she's saying is that she wants a chance to race?"

They both stood where they were, silent and frustrated. If he'd had his way, Heath would have marched up to Barbie, taken her in his arms, and kissed her until things were better between them. He'd been convinced they'd reached a new understanding in their relationship the other day, but now he didn't know where he stood. He had to do something to solve the impasse they'd stumbled into.

"I can try," he said, spreading his arms wide.

She nodded, then pulled herself up into the saddle. "And I can try to do everything in my power to make sure I don't push Daisy, or myself, too hard."

He nodded in return. The two of them held their ground, him standing and her sitting atop Daisy, for several long seconds.

At last, she let out a breath. "I do love you, Heath. You know that."

"And I love you," he replied, no idea why saying it made him feel so helpless.

"Let's just leave it there for now," she went on. "We can talk about it all again when we've worked off some steam."

"Okay." He sighed, no idea if he was doing the right thing or caving in when he shouldn't. "You and Daisy be careful out there."

Of all things, she smiled, even if it was a watery smile. She nudged Daisy and turned her to head out to the paddock gate. Heath walked with them, opening the gate when he reached it so that they could all pass through. Once Daisy and Barbie took off toward the barrel course, he didn't head back to the stable. He had too much on his mind, too much to sort through, which meant there was only one thing he could do.

8

The Langley house truly felt like a home to Heath, and home was where he wanted to be at that moment, with all the confusion of life and love swirling around him. He was certain he'd find his dad puttering around the house somewhere, and sure enough, as soon as he was through the kitchen door, he heard the tell-tale sound of a jigsaw buzzing away in the basement.

Aidan Langley had been through a lot, and as soon as Heath descended into the basement, spotting his dad hard at work, cutting out whatever new woodworking project he'd taken up, he smiled. If anyone could help him sort through the jumble, it was his dad. The man had a quiet confidence and gave off vibes of peace and happiness. For a few seconds, Heath just stood at the bottom of the steps, watching him work. Part of him wanted to shake his head at how together his dad was. He'd never have things half so figured out.

At last, Aidan turned off the saw and pushed his work goggles up to his forehead. "You just gonna stand there itching, son, or are you gonna tell me what's bothering you?"

Heath laughed softly and pushed away from the stairs. "Is it that obvious?"

Aidan turned his work stool to face Heath, shrugging. "You've just come home from a war. You lost your best friend. You're dating a headstrong woman." He paused, a grin pulling at the corner of his mouth. "You and Barbie are dating now, aren't you?"

"Yeah." Heath drew out the syllable.

Aidan huffed a laugh. "So it's girl problems, is it?"

Heath sighed, slumping into the old sofa that had been moved to the basement when he was a kid. "It's everything, dad. Everything. And I don't know what to do about any of it."

Aidan made a sympathetic noise and got up to join Heath on the sofa. "Talk to me."

Heath rubbed a hand over his face, his emotions so jumbled up that he didn't know where to start.

The only thing he could think of to say was, "The world isn't the same place that it was two years ago."

Aidan chuckled, shaking his head. "The world is never the same place it was. That's the thing about the world. It's always changing, always throwing new challenges at us." He tilted his head to the side. "It's always coming up with great new stuff too."

"Maybe." Heath leaned back, already feeling better, but still confused. "I just wish I could keep up."

"Is it Barbie?" Aidan asked, studying him with wise eyes. "Because I know a lot of the guys on the ranch have a hard time accepting her authority as their boss. But she's excellent at what she does, son, and you shouldn't go interfering with her."

"That's not it," Heath said, but a flash of heat up his neck and the sudden inability to meet his father's eyes told another story. "At least I don't think it is," he added. He wanted to be honest with himself, and that started with being completely honest with his dad. "I'm proud of everything Barbie's accomplished, and I like the way she seems so driven."

"You just wish she'd be driven with everyone else but defer to you?" Aidan guessed.

Heath winced. "No. Maybe. I hope not." He let out a breath. "It's this whole thing with Daisy," he said with a burst of energy. "She keeps insisting that she's going to enter Davy's horse in competitions."

"She's not Davy's horse anymore," Aidan pointed out. "She belongs to the both of you."

"Yeah, and I don't want to see Daisy hurt. Barrel racing can be dangerous. You've seen the way some of those horses go down if they try to take the turns too tightly or if the rider pushes the horse too far."

"Are you concerned that Barbie would push Daisy too far?"

Heath frowned. He had to be honest. "Not exactly. I know she and Daisy have a special bond, and Barbie keeps insisting racing is what Daisy wants."

"So where's the problem?"

"I don't want Daisy to get hurt," Heath answered immediately. "I keep seeing visions of her breaking a leg when she misjudges a turn. It's like I can hear her screaming in my head. What would we all do if she hurt herself so badly that we had to put—" He stopped, his throat closing up before he could finish. The image of Davy's confused, bloody and sweaty face right after he'd been shot popped into Heath's head.

Aidan kept silent for several long seconds, watching Heath with a look of such compassion that it brought him close to tears. At last, he said, "Son, it's not Daisy you're worried about."

More silence followed. Heath leaned forward, resting his elbows on his knees and burying his face in his hands. He knew full well that the deal with Daisy was all about Davy. He also knew there wasn't a damn thing he could do about it.

"I want to ask Barbie to marry me," he said at last, glancing up at his dad. "She knows I'm going to ask at some point, and I think she'll say yes."

"You *think?*"

He winced. "We sort of just had a fight down in the stable."

"So?" Aidan shrugged. "Fights happen. Your mom and I have had a few in our days." A fond grin spread across his face.

"Yeah, but this one was...." He couldn't put his finger on the words to describe the issues between him and Barbie. Issues that couldn't be easily resolved. "She doesn't want to quit her job if we have kids."

Of all things, Aidan chuckled. "Of course she doesn't."

Heath sat straighter in surprise. "You don't sound like you think that's a bad thing."

"Why does it have to be a bad thing?"

"Because that's not what women do. That's not what Mom did."

Aidan shook his head and leaned forward. "This is what I mean about the world constantly changing. Women are doing amazing things right now, and why not? Your mom is smarter than I am. Who's to say that Barbie isn't smarter than you? And if she's good at her job, which she is, why should being a woman, or even a mother, stop her from doing that job?"

Heath let out a breath and slumped against the back of the sofa. "This isn't the way I imagined my life turning out."

"Son, no one's life turns out the way they imagine it." Aidan sat back as well, shaking his head. "That's what life is all about."

Heath frowned, staring at the pile of sawdust on the floor under his dad's workbench. "I always thought that Davy would grow old along with me and Barbie. I thought that our kids would be friends. I thought he'd be here." His throat started to close up again, and his eyes stung.

"Losing a friend is always hard," Aidan said, quiet but steady. "Especially the way you lost Davy. But Davy wouldn't want you to grind your life to a halt just because he's not there. And he'd want Barbie to be happy too."

"I keep trying to ask myself what Davy would have wanted for Daisy. He loved that horse."

"We all know that." Aidan nodded. "She wouldn't have made it past that first night if he hadn't poured his heart and soul into caring for her. But I think he wouldn't want her to be cooped up in a paddock all the time, unable to do anything she wanted to either."

Heath glanced to his dad. "You're saying I should let Barbie race Daisy."

Aidan chuckled. "Son, I'm saying you don't have a choice in the matter. The ladies have you outvoted. All you can do is sit back and make peace with the way things are." He stood, thumping Heath's knee as he did, and headed back to his workbench.

One last thing stuck in Heath's heart, unable to wrestle free. "Dad, ever since I came back from Vietnam, I don't know where I fit. Nothing is the way it used to be."

Aidan hummed and nodded. "The men who came back from Europe and the Pacific all those years ago had the same problem. I never did serve, but I remember how it was for them coming back. Every man who goes off to war comes back asking the same questions you're asking. Who am I? Where do I belong now?"

"And what are the answers?"

Aidan grinned at him and picked up his goggles. "I can't answer that for you, son. But I can tell you this much, the answer is not to make other people into who you think they should be."

"I'm not trying to make anyone into anything," Heath protested.

"No?" Aidan raised a brow. "You sure you're not trying to make Barbie into someone like your mother, or Daisy into an invalid when she's not?"

Heath let out a breath as the questions struck home. Maybe he was fighting to mold the world into the image he wanted it to be. But if that were true, it was only because he needed something to hold onto, something stable and recognizable. He couldn't keep wading through the swamps and jungles of a foreign land anymore. But if his dad was right, maybe the solution to the knots that wouldn't leave his stomach was to learn the new terrain of home.

The only thing worse to Barbie than arguing with Heath was the gnawing sense that she'd overreacted. For days, she couldn't shake the notion that maybe she should have been more accommodating to Heath, maybe she shouldn't have been so stubborn or put her foot down so hard. She prized her freedom and the role Aidan Langley had given her at his ranch, but the insidious thought that maybe she should be a little more feminine and give in to Heath kept her up at night. Especially since Heath *wasn't* there keeping her up at night.

They'd seen each other a few times since their fight. Heath had apologized for getting upset, and she'd done the same. They'd kissed and made up, but a lot of things had remained unsaid. Too many. Since they hadn't gone out after work or snuck off to make out or done any of the things that had made her so giddy on and after the Fourth of July, she knew the issues between them were still there. They were both busy with their own things, but Barbie was certain she knew what the real problem was. The race.

"You sure you want to do this?" she whispered to Daisy as she brushed her in preparation for saddling her at the rodeo arena on the morning of the race. "We don't have to prove anything, you know. Heath can see that you're a good, strong horse."

Daisy nickered and bobbed her head. She

stomped a foot, giving Barbie the impression that she would race or be in a snit for weeks.

"Okay, then, girl." She couldn't help but smile at the answer as she stroked Daisy's sides. "I knew you were a fighter."

"That's what Davy always said."

Barbie looked up to find Mrs. Sudgeon standing a few yards away. She wore a handsome skirt suit, like she always did, which looked utterly out of place in the dusty staging area of the rodeo. Her pillbox hat was perfectly centered atop immaculately coifed hair. If Barbie hadn't known any better, she'd have thought Davy's mom was on her way to church.

"Hey, Mrs. Sudgeon. I didn't see you standing there," Barbie said. She gave Daisy's side a pat, then walked up to face Mrs. Sudgeon, nervous energy coursing through her. "Have you come to watch the race?"

Mrs. Sudgeon gave a small nod, then stepped over to stroke Daisy's nose with her gloved hand. "Davy always used to say she was a fighter. She didn't give up that night when she was born."

"Davy had a lot to do with that," Barbie admitted. She tossed the brush she'd been using aside and moved to stand by Mrs. Sudgeon's side. "He fought for her."

Mrs. Sudgeon nodded. There was so much sadness in her eyes as she pet Daisy that Barbie's throat closed up. She couldn't imagine the kind of loss the woman had been through.

"Mrs. Sudgeon," she asked, suddenly anxious, shifting her weight from one foot to the other. "Do you think I'm doing the right thing?"

Mrs. Sudgeon's brow lifted. "The right thing, dear?"

"By racing Daisy," Barbie said. She hugged herself, not sure why she felt more awkward asking Davy's mom about the whole thing than Heath. "Heath thinks it could be dangerous, that Daisy could get hurt."

Mrs. Sudgeon blinked. "Why would he? You've been working with Daisy for years. And you're a good rider."

Barbie let out a breath, drooping with relief. It was far stronger than she anticipated. "Thank you." She reached out to stroke Daisy's neck. "I keep feeling like this is what Daisy wants to do, but I'm having a hard time convincing Heath of that."

"Well, he's got a lot on his plate, doesn't he?" Mrs. Sudgeon answered, looking down. The grief in her eyes seemed to grow.

Barbie stepped over and hugged her, not even

sure why, other than that she felt it was the right thing to do. "We've all got a lot on our plates," she said. "I guess...I guess that's why I feel so strongly about racing Daisy. But at the same time, I hate going against what Heath wants."

To her surprise, Mrs. Sudgeon let out a soft laugh. "That's the thing I don't understand about you modern girls. Back in my day, if our man wanted something, we'd do it. No matter what."

"No offense, but I can't even imagine doing that," Barbie said.

Mrs. Sudgeon smiled and shook her head. "And that's what I don't understand. I would have done anything for peace and happiness when I was your age. And all the magazines said the same thing. If your man is happy, you'll be happy."

Barbie's face pinched with doubt before she could stop it. "You don't really believe that, do you?"

Mrs. Sudgeon shrugged and went back to stroking Daisy's nose. "It worked for me. For a while. We were all happy." Her hand stopped moving. "And then we weren't. And it wasn't my decision."

"I'm so sorry," Barbie whispered.

Silence fell between them. Mrs. Sudgeon continued to stare at Daisy, and, to her credit, Daisy stared back with patience and compassion. Barbie had the sudden sense that she was an intruder in someone else's intimate conversation, that, in their hearts, Daisy and Mrs. Sudgeon were coming to some sort of understanding. More than that, she had the eerie sense that Daisy was speaking for Davy.

After a silence so long it left prickles down Barbie's back, Mrs. Sudgeon said, "I think Davy would be proud to watch Daisy race. I think he would have loved to be here today."

"Me too," Barbie whispered, blinking rapidly to fight back tears. "I just wish Heath could understand that."

"Understand what?"

Barbie gasped and turned to see Heath striding toward them. He wore jeans and a simple, button-down shirt. His face was a little wan, even though he smiled at her, as though he carried the weight of the world on his shoulders.

"Mrs. Sudgeon." He greeted Davy's mom with a respectful nod. Tension rippled off him.

Mrs. Sudgeon smiled at him, then glanced to Barbie. "I think the two of you have things you need to talk about," she said in a quiet voice. "I'll leave you to it."

"You don't have to go," Barbie said, hating the

idea that someone so important to her and to Heath would feel like they were in the way.

"It's all right, dear," she said, then smiled at Heath. "It's all right."

She squeezed his arm as she passed, leaving the two of them alone.

9

Restless anxiety rippled through Heath, turning his gut to jelly as he watched Barbie. She looked beautiful in riding gear. Her jeans fit like a glove and the vest she wore over a checkered shirt was both feminine and made her look like she knew what she was doing. But it was the way she crossed her arms, shifted her weight to one leg, and stared at him, waiting, that made him swallow and rub a hand over his face.

"Were you talking to Davy's mom?" he asked the stupid, obvious question, mostly because he didn't know how else to articulate what he wanted to say.

"She's really supportive," Barbie answered.

"Yeah, she always was."

Silence fell between them. Heath hated every second of it. There was so much he needed to say, so many things that had been rolling around in his heart and his head since talking to his dad. Heck, they had been jumbled up, looking for a way to be said since Vietnam.

At last, he cleared his throat and toed the dirt of the arena's staging area. "I want things to be okay between us," he said.

"That's what I want too," Barbie said, her voice soft. She took a step toward him, bit her lip, and looked as though she would reach out for him. At the last minute, she held back. "Please, please tell me that you didn't come back here to try to talk me out of racing Daisy today." Her eyes filled with pleading. They also filled with hope.

Heath took a long breath. His head told him one thing, but his heart argued the other. Through it all, his heart pounded against his ribs like the chop of helicopter blades. Whether that chopper was coming to rescue him or abandon him, he didn't know.

"I wish that I could let my fears go and send you into this race with my full blessing," he started, his gut clenching when he reached the word "fears".

"Heath, this is something I have to do," she said with a disappointed sigh, her shoulders dropping. "I know you don't approve, but—"

Heath held up his hands to stop her.

"I know. I'm not going to stop you from racing."

Barbie blinked. "You're not?"

He shook his head. "Look, I love you." A splash of color came to her face and hope filled her expression. "I want you to be happy," he went on. "And I know that you have a lot of ideas that are different from mine. You see a lot of things in ways that I don't."

"If you're talking about Daisy," she said, glancing quickly to their horse, "all I ask is that you trust me to know what I'm doing."

"I do. Believe me, I do."

Heath took a deep breath. It shouldn't have been so hard for him to express his emotions, but he was so desperate to get things right, to prevent any more conflict or sorrow from happening that every word he spoke seemed to take on way too much significance.

"I talked to dad about it, and I've watched you for the past few days," he went on. "You and Daisy really do have a great partnership. And no matter what idiots like Rick think, Dad promises me that you're on top of everything at the ranch and know what you're doing. I can see that too."

Barbie shifted as though she didn't quite know what to make of his words. "Thanks. I've worked hard." She glanced to Daisy. "We've both worked hard."

"Which is why I think you should race."

Barbie's eyebrows shot up. "You think we *should* race? That's different from not stopping me from racing."

He hadn't quite thought of it that way, but she was right. "I think it's what Davy would have wanted," he said slowly.

A grin spread across Barbie's face. "Mrs. Sudgeon just said the same thing."

In spite of the maelstrom of emotions inside of him, Heath smiled. "Did she? Then it must be true."

Barbie took a step toward him, grasping his hands. "You can trust me, Heath. I know how much you care about Daisy. I know how she...." She lowered her eyes and took a breath before glancing up at him. "We both think of Daisy as the part of Davy that's left. I know what you went through when Davy died, and I just want you to know that I will do everything in my power to keep Daisy from being hurt the way...." She let her words trail off again and glanced to the side.

"It's okay," Heath forced himself to say. "I'm going to need to find a way to talk about Davy's death with people eventually. Dad helped me to see that the more I hold on to everything that happened over there, the harder it's going to be for me to find where I fit back home now."

Barbie's smile widened. "Your dad said that?"

"Well, no, not exactly, but that's what I took from it."

"In that case, you and your dad are both really smart guys."

Her smile reached her eyes, and even though there were no fireworks or trumpets sounding, Heath felt as though they'd reached a new level and a good place in their relationship. His gut was still in knots, especially when the announcement came over the loudspeaker that all barrel racing participants needed to report to the starting area, but his heart wasn't as overwhelmed as it had been for months.

"You'd better go," he said, nodding to the area where the other racers were gathering. "You and Daisy don't want to miss your big chance."

"We won't." She squeezed his hands, then stepped over to Daisy. "Come on, girl."

She stepped into the stirrups and mounted, sitting so easily in Daisy's saddle that Heath wondered how he could ever have questioned her skill or confidence. Barbie knew what she was doing.

She probably knew what she was doing in every aspect of her life, far more than he ever had.

"We can do this," she said, smiling at him.

Whether she meant the race or so much more, Heath didn't know, but he nodded in return and patted Daisy's side as Barbie walked past. "We can."

He watched her walk off, joining the others. As much as he wanted everything to be sunshine and roses, his smile dropped and his nerves raged as she spoke to one of the race officials. Heath took a deep breath and forced himself not to run after her and demand she change her mind. He turned, put one foot in front of the other, and headed from the staging area out to the stands.

His parents were already watching the earlier rodeo events, and Davy's parents were sitting with them. As Heath took the seat they had reserved for him, Mrs. Sudgeon treated him to a proud smile. As Heath settled in beside her, eyes on the arena as the announcer introduced the first barrel-racing competitor, she leaned over and whispered, "I'm so proud of you."

Heath blinked and turned to face her. "Me? I didn't do anything."

Mrs. Sudgeon took his hand and squeezed it.

"You did so much." Her eyes were large and misty, which caused Heath's throat to close up.

"I feel like I haven't done anything since getting home," he confessed.

She shook her head. "You've done more than you know. Barbie is just glowing these days."

"I don't think I have anything to do with that." Heath tried to laugh and make light of things.

"The two of you were born to be together," Mrs. Sudgeon went on. "I was worried that Davy's death would come between you, but I was wrong. He would be over the moon about how close the two of you have gotten."

"I—" Heath's throat closed up before he could find an answer. Davy would have gotten a kick out of the way he and Barbie had finally gotten on with things. He'd teased Heath about going home and marrying her all the time out there in the jungle.

He opened his mouth to try again to reply to Mrs. Sudgeon, but he still had no words, and the announcer brought every thought and attempt at conversation to a halt as he announced, "Our first competitor in today's barrel race are June Withers and Bella!"

Heath's attention snapped to the dusty arena as the crowd swelled with applause. It wasn't even

Barbie's turn to compete, but as the excitement in the arena built, his adrenaline levels kicked up. With that came the old familiar dread and anticipation of battle. Something was coming, and it might not be good.

"Stop being such a nervous Nelly," Davy's voice echoed in his memory. "We're here to do a job. Three hours from now, we'll be back here changing into dry socks and laughing over nothing."

He'd said the same thing every time they went out on patrol. He'd said it the night he didn't come back. Davy's teasing smile and easy laugh echoed in Heath's memory with a blend of fondness and regret.

As soon as the starter's pistol went off, he jumped. The horse and rider in the arena launched into motion, tearing around the barrel course as the crowd cheered them on. People jumped to their feet, waving arms and hats, but Heath was glued to his seat. It wasn't until the first racer finished the course that he realized he was still holding Mrs. Sudgeon's hand and squeezing it far too hard.

"Sorry," he murmured, pulling out of her grip.

Mrs. Sudgeon smiled at him and blinked her watery eyes. "It's okay, son."

Son. The word should have been Davy's and Davy's alone, but it struck Heath's heart like an arrow, spreading warmth through him. He reached for Mrs. Sudgeon's hand again, taking a deep breath.

It was painful to sit through racers waiting for Barbie. Each time the starter's pistol went off, a flood of memories returned. Heath wondered if it would ever get easier, if he would ever be able to enjoy fireworks again. He'd loved loud, sharp noises as a kid, and would have given anything to reclaim the innocence of those fun days.

And then it was time.

"Our next competitors are Barbie Rose and Daisy," the announcer called out.

The group of spectators from New Dawn Springs swelled with cheers. Every one of them must have known that Barbie was racing Davy's horse, racing in his honor. For her part, Barbie stayed focused on the course in front of her when she appeared at the starting line. She leaned low over Daisy's neck, whispering something to her. Heath swallowed hard and forced himself to breathe, forced himself to face what he was terrified of.

The starting pistol cracked, and he jumped. Barbie and Daisy shot into action, zooming toward the first barrel. Heath's heart leapt into his throat and stayed there. The reverberation of the pistol expanded in his ears as memories of machine gun fire and exploding grenades drowned out the cheers and hollers of the crowd. Davy was right there with him, facing the unseen enemy in the dark. The two of them were together, advancing, firing, pulling back, like they had in so many other skirmishes before. Brothers in arms. Neither would be left behind.

The crowd swelled as Barbie and Daisy rounded the first barrel. Heath watched, but the sight in front of him was eclipsed by the visions from his memory. Davy, smiling one second, shot through the throat the next. The scent of blood seemed to fill his nose. The cheers around him sounded like shouted orders, the confused cries of terrified and wounded soldiers. The noise was deafening, pressing in on him and dragging him under.

Barbie and Daisy rounded the second barrel. Davy. He had to save Davy. He had to carry him back to safety, wipe away the blood. Davy would snap out of it, smile, and tell him he'd been teasing. But the shouting and firing continued, the darkness closed in, the heat and humidity and stink of the jungle choked him. He had to do something. He had to—

The crowd gasped, and Heath snapped back to the present moment. Every nerve in his body flared with panic. Barbie and Daisy headed into the third barrel, but something went wrong. Daisy was falling, her legs flailing. Barbie was thrown to the side, and in the split-second it took for Daisy to right herself, she flew from the saddle.

Heath leapt to his feet, numb and shaking. His heart stopped. He couldn't breathe. All he could do was watch. Watch as Barbie sprawled in the dirt of the race course. Watch as she rolled slowly to her side, pushing herself to her hands and knees in obvious pain. Watch as she struggled to stand, holding her arms out to regain her balance. Half the rest of the crowd was on their feet as well, but they faded into the background. All noise faded into nothing but the steady pounding of Heath's pulse in his ears.

And then Barbie reached down and slapped the dust from her jeans. She turned and searched for Daisy, who was bobbing her head just a few yards away. Barbie whistled, and Daisy leapt over to her, still full of energy, still ready to go. Barbie grabbed hold of the saddle, stuck her foot in the stirrup, and swung herself up.

The crowd cheered as she settled herself atop Daisy, but Heath barely heard any of it. He watched, eyes wide, as Barbie wheeled Daisy around, leaned over, tapped her sides, then raced around the last barrel one more time. The crowd cheered as Daisy shot toward the finish line. Her stride was clean and even. If she'd been hurt in the fall, she didn't show it.

"That's my girl," Aidan shouted to Heath's right.

Heath blinked, glancing sideways at his father. The man was beaming, tears in his eyes, as he applauded Barbie and Daisy's finish. Emotion stronger than he ever would have suspected he'd feel gripped Heath. He could only pray that he'd be able to support Barbie as thoroughly and selflessly as his father.

The crowd cheered in spite of the ruined run, but Heath ignored it. He pushed his way down the row of seats and into the aisle, breaking into a run when he reached the stairs. All he could think about was the way Barbie had fallen, and the way she had gotten up. If she was hurt, he needed to go to her. Heck, he needed to go to her either way.

## 10

Barbie winced as she rode Daisy back to the holding area behind the competition arena. She could feel bruises forming all along one side where she'd hit the ground as Daisy tripped. It hadn't been a hard fall, but any fall was painful. Ironically, her shoulder hurt more than anything else, not because it had hit the dirt with the rest of her, but because she'd tried to hold on, concentrating on Daisy when she should have been breaking her fall. She'd yanked all the muscles in her right shoulder trying to make sure Daisy was safe.

"You okay, girl?" she asked as they came to a stop in front of the stall where their things were stored. Barbie dismounted gingerly, wincing as she did. But she didn't care how many bruises she had or how long it would take to heal, Daisy was her only concern.

She did a quick check, running her hands over Daisy's forelegs, then moving to the back and checking for anything that didn't look right.

"Is she okay? Is she hurt?"

Barbie's heart rose in her chest, then fell flat as Rick, not Heath, came striding toward the stall. She rubbed her face to hide her souring expression, then sighed. "Yeah. I keep telling everyone she's a tough girl. She bounced right back up when we went down."

"I'll be the judge of that," Rick grumbled as he reached Daisy and began his examination. As distasteful as Barbie found the man, he was trained in equine medicine. He knew what he was looking for and how to assess injuries. With any luck, he'd avoid being a jerk about it too.

Daisy nickered and reached her nose toward Barbie. Barbie managed a weak smile and shook herself out of the gloom that was trying to press down on her. She stepped closer to Daisy, stroking her neck and resting her head against Daisy's forehead.

"I'm sorry, girl," she said, closing her eyes and

cradling Daisy's head. "I know you wanted to run. I let you down."

"You didn't let anyone down."

Barbie sucked in a breath and turned. That was the voice she wanted to hear, and sure enough, Heath was standing just a few feet behind her. He looked worn and ragged, with a little more color in his face than should have been there, even if he'd run from the stands.

"Are you all right?" he asked, closing the distance between them and reaching out for her.

"More or less," she replied with a self-deprecating smile. "It wasn't a hard fall, but I've probably got more than my share of bruises under these jeans. And I know what you're going to say, I shouldn't have—"

Before she could finish, Heath pulled her into his arms, planting a passionate kiss on her lips. She was so taken by surprise that she gave in, opening her mouth to his and letting him surround her, envelope her. His arms held her up, and the intensity of the way he held her knocked the hat right off her head.

As the shock wore off, the pain of her bruises and her shoulder flared. She moaned against Heath's mouth, but not in the good way. Moments later, he let her go.

"You are hurt," he said, then quickly added, "Sorry. I shouldn't have grabbed you like that."

"Believe me, it's okay," Barbie panted. Her heart showed no signs of beating any less furiously. Her lips tingled, and she could still taste Heath. Something had changed between them, she could feel it. All she wanted to do was wrap herself up in his arms and explore what it could be, but her body was nowhere near ready for that.

"Do you need to see the medic?" Heath asked, then shook his head and said, "The doctor. Or the nurse. Whatever it is they have at events like this."

"No, it's just bruises and my shoulder," she said, then rushed on. "I'm sorry, Heath."

He blinked and stared at her. "Sorry? For what?"

"You were right. Daisy and I weren't ready for something like this. We needed more training. I just wanted to prove that both of us could do it."

Behind them, Rick snorted. Both Barbie and Heath ignored him, though the sound of disapproval instantly made Barbie want to take back everything she'd just said. With guys like Rick around, she did need to prove herself.

Heath surprised her by saying, "You were brilliant."

Barbie's jaw dropped. She studied him, looking

for some indication that he was teasing her or that he was about to turn around and tell her he'd told her so. But instead of some kind of hidden agenda, Heath merely stared at her with a look of pride. "I wasn't brilliant," she said at last. "I pushed Daisy too hard around that last turn. I didn't trust her instincts enough. She didn't have to go down."

"But she wasn't hurt," Heath said, then raised an eyebrow. "Was she?"

Barbie shook her head, shooting a look over her shoulder to where Rick was finishing up his exam. "I don't think so. She's probably got a few bruises, just like me, but that's it."

"Good."

"You were right, though," Barbie sighed, bending to pick up her hat with a wince.

"No." Heath took her hat from her and tossed it aside before sliding his arms around her. "You were the one who was right."

As odd as it felt to have him agree with her, she couldn't argue with the warmth of his arms, or the way standing so close to him made her feel stronger. "Are you sure *you're* all right?" she asked.

Heath took a deep breath. "I don't know."

Strangely enough, that admission filled Barbie

with relief far more than him declaring he was fine would have.

He frowned, the look in his eyes suddenly distant. "Out there, watching you race...it brought up a lot of memories." He paused. She could tell without asking what those memories were. He'd been thinking of Davy, thinking of the war.

"I'm sorry," she said softly when he didn't continue. "I wish I'd been there with you."

Heath's eyes focused, and he smiled at her. "You were busy doing your thing. And, as it turns out, your thing is pretty amazing."

She arched an eyebrow. "Wiping out and nearly injuring myself and Davy's horse in the process?"

He only flinched a little at Davy's name. "Getting up," he said. "The way you recovered, the way you didn't let a fall keep you down or stop you from finishing the course." He took a long, deep breath as if steadying himself. "It was amazing."

Everything suddenly made sense. Whether he'd been waiting for someone to show him that it was possible to pick yourself up from a fall and continue on or whether everything had come to him at once, it didn't matter. He'd turned a corner.

"And you were right about Daisy being strong,"

he went on, looking slightly embarrassed. "I don't know why I was so stuck on her being delicate."

"Because that's the way she was when you and Davy left," Barbie said. "It took a lot of work to get her where she is now, but she was willing to do that work."

"I'm willing to do that work too," he said, barely above a whisper, as if the idea both scared him and filled him with hope. "Everything has changed. The world before the war, the world with Davy in it, was a different place from the world as it is now, but I'm ready to figure out where I fit in this world. As long as I'm with you when I do it."

Joy filled Barbie's heart in a way she never could have anticipated. Her smile widened, and in spite of her aches and pains, she circled her arms around Heath and squeezed him tight. "We'll figure this out together."

He hugged her back, kissing the top of her head, then brushing his fingers along her chin and tilting her face up so that he could kiss her lips. It was a wonderful kiss, filled with hope and promise. Barbie never wanted it to end, even though they were in a crowded, public arena.

"I like the look of that," Rick interrupted them, his tone seedy enough to change Barbie's mind about kissing in public. "That's what a woman should be doing."

Heath's body went rigid, and he let Barbie go in order to face Rick. "Excuse me?"

Rick sent him a smarmy grin. "Hey, I'm on your side, man."

"What do you mean, 'my side'?" Heath narrowed his eyes.

Rick shrugged. "I suppose racing is okay, but women were meant for kissing and cooking, not running a ranch."

"What does running a ranch have to do with anything?" Barbie asked, crossing her arms.

"Well...." Rick glanced from Barbie to Heath, his grin faltering. "I just figure that, now that the two of you are kissing in public and all, you'll get married."

"Whether we do or not is none of your business," Heath said.

"And it still has nothing to do with running a ranch," Barbie added.

Rick shifted from smarmy self-confidence to narrow-eyed defensiveness. "Not this clap-trap about women being able to do a man's job again."

"Hey." Heath rounded on Rick, backing him against the stall wall. "I'm sick of listening to you put

Barbie, and all women, down. A job's a job, no matter who does it."

"You can't possibly believe that." Rick tried one last time to sneer and look superior, but his grin died before it could fully form as Heath stared at him, unblinking. "You've gotta want your job as ranch manager back," he said, uncertainty twitching in his expression.

"Legacy Ranch already has a manager," Heath said. "And a damn fine one at that. My father hired the best, and I intend to stick with the staff he has."

Barbie smiled. She'd never doubted Heath would let her stay in her job, but up until that moment, she hadn't realized how much he supported her. It felt good, better than winning any trophies could.

"I'll tell you what's more," Heath went on, smiling at Barbie and sliding an arm around her waist. "If she'll have me, then I will marry her." Butterflies filled Barbie's stomach. They'd talked about marriage, but it hadn't felt so real until that moment. "And what's more," Heath went on, "if things go the way Mom and Dad and Kevin have talked about, I'll inherit the ranch someday, since Kevin likes city life so much. And that means that Barbie won't just manage it, she'll own it too."

Ripples of excitement zipped through Barbie,

but they had nothing to do with owning Legacy Ranch. She could see far more than a business partnership in Heath's eyes. She could see love there, a future, children and grandchildren. She thought of the wedding dress Maura had showed her in the Langley house's attic, the antique lace with its long, long history. She stood to become a part of that history, and nothing had ever felt more wonderful.

"Suit yourself," Rick grumbled, slinking past them, his hands shoved in his pockets. "I'd never marry a woman as uptight and presumptuous as that."

"Honestly, I don't see any woman giving you the time of day," Heath drawled as Rick walked away.

Rick snorted and made a rude gesture, keeping his back to the two of them. A burst of anger filled Barbie, but it wasn't worth it to pursue the matter.

"If he ever gives you any trouble, just let me know and I'll take care of it," Heath said.

Barbie grinned as she turned to face him. "Honey, if he ever gives me any trouble, I'll fire his ass before you even get there to help me."

Heath laughed. The sound was surprising and beautiful. But not half as beautiful as the ease Barbie could feel in his body when he took her in his arms again.

"You really are something else, you know," he said, then added, "Davy would have gotten such a kick out of watching you set Rick straight. He would have loved to see you and Daisy race today too."

"I know." Barbie's throat felt suddenly tight. "I'm sure he was watching today from wherever he is."

"And I know he'll be watching next time you race."

Barbie's brow shot up. "You mean, you'd be okay with Daisy and I trying again? After all that stuff you've been saying for the past few weeks?"

Heath sighed, resting his forehead against hers for a moment. "I can't keep living my life like it's thirty seconds before Davy is shot and I might be able to change what happened if I do things right. Davy died for his country. That's what he wanted. But I'm starting to see that now I need to live for him and for what he believed in."

Tears stung at Barbie's eyes. She blinked them back as she leaned into Heath, hugging him for all she was worth. "We'll be okay," she whispered. "Even without him, we'll be okay."

"I know." Heath closed his arms around her. "Maybe it won't be easy, and I'm sure there will be days when I can't take it. But as long as I have you with me, I can go on. We can go on."

"And we will," Barbie said. She leaned back enough to kiss him, circling her arms around his neck. She couldn't imagine her life without Heath, troubles and all, and she vowed that the two of them would face everything that came their way, everything that would rear up out of the past too, together.

EPILOGUE

NEW DAWN SPRINGS – 1990

Time healed all wounds, but it still left scars behind. Heath paced the halls of the hospital, remembering all the other times he'd been trapped with the sounds of medical machines, the smells of antiseptic, and the interminable wait that only the most extreme moments of life brought with it.

He thought about that horrible time in Vietnam, when he'd woken up in the hospital to the news that Davy hadn't made it. Somewhere in his subconscious, he'd hoped everything he'd experienced on the battle field was just a dream and Davy would be there, but it wasn't meant to be.

He remembered the time six months after he married Barbie when she had fallen off of Daisy while riding out to search for a stray mare and she'd been rushed to the hospital. He'd been beside himself with fear, but the doctor had come out of the examination room to tell him that not only was Barbie just fine, the reason she'd fallen was because she was pregnant and her balance was off.

He remembered that brilliant, beautiful moment seven months later, when another doctor had stepped out of the delivery room to announce that he had a son, and the tear-filled moment shortly after when he and Barbie had unanimously agreed to name the baby David.

He remembered several other trips to the hospital too, three girls, and then another boy. Times had changed by the time Patrick was born, and he'd been allowed into the delivery room for his second son's birth. Although by that point, Barbie was a pro and hardly needed his help.

Heath also remembered the sorrowful day that the whole family had gathered in the hospital to say goodbye to his father when, after a good, long, life, his heart finally gave out and he went on to his greater reward.

There'd been other, minor trips to the hospital

too—when David broke his arm falling from a tree, when his daughter, Emma, had had the croup so bad they'd rushed her to the emergency room, when another daughter, Maura, earned her medical degree and they'd all accompanied her to her first shift in the ER—but Heath's reasons for going to the hospital that morning were perhaps the best of all.

"Quit your pacing, old man," Barbie teased him, shaking her head and continuing with her knitting. She still looked as beautiful as the day he'd married her as she sat in the waiting room chair, an expectant smile on her face.

"Easy for you to say," he grumbled. He sounded more and more like his father with each passing year. The only consolation to that was that David sounded more and more like him as he grew older.

As if thinking of his son made him appear, David burst through the door from the delivery room. Heath caught his breath, and Barbie rose from her chair, tossing her knitting aside.

"Here he is," David announced with a proud smile, tilting up the blue bundle in his arms to give Heath and Barbie a look. "Meet the newest chapter in the Langley family legacy, Collin Langley."

Tears stung at Heath's eyes, even though he promised himself he wouldn't cry. He'd waited a long time for a grandchild, though, and at last, here he was. He took a tentative step forward.

"He's awful quiet for a little guy who's just made his way into the world," he said.

"He's probably tired after all that labor," David laughed.

"How's Monica?" Barbie asked.

"She's doing just fine," David told them. "She came through like a champ." He paused, taking a step closer to Heath. "Would you like to hold him, Dad?"

Heath's heart skipped a beat, and he grinned from ear to ear. "Would I ever!"

He held out his arms, and David gently transferred the newborn over to him. It'd been years since Heath had held a baby, but he'd done his fair share while raising his and Barbie's five kids, and it all came back to him. Better still, as soon as Collin was nestled safely in his arms, he opened his eyes and squinted up at Heath.

"Hey there, little guy," Heath said, his voice far hoarser than usual. "I'm your grandpa. You can call me Pappy."

"No, Heath," Barbie said with a humorous sigh, shaking her head. "We discussed this. The grandkids are *not* going to call you Pappy."

"Why not? It's a cool name." Heath looked up at David and winked. "Isn't 'cool' what all the kids are saying these days."

"Sure, Dad," David laughed.

Heath chuckled and looked at the perfect, blue bundle in his arms again. "Stick with me, kid," he said, "Pappy'll take real good care of you. You and I are gonna have a good time."

He could feel it all the way through his old bones. Collin was a special one, and he would do anything to make sure he had the happiest life possible. The Langley legacy had a long way yet to go.

---

I HOPE YOU'VE ENJOYED READING *Heath's Homecoming*! It was bittersweet doing research for this book. I'll admit that my knowledge of the Vietnam era wasn't what it should have been when I set myself the task of writing about a returning vet. I owe a huge debt of gratitude to Kevin Burns and Lynn Novik's documentary series, *The Vietnam War*, which aired on PBS in 2017. It was difficult to watch, I had to take it in small doses and break it up with happier entertainment, but I feel like they did a really good job of presenting all sides of the war and its aftermath. I also wanted to convey attitudes about women in *Heath's Homecoming* that were prevalent at the time, but that frustrated a lot of us now. I hope I've succeeded!

And now, be sure to pick up the last book in the series, *Collin's Challenge*, by Sylvia McDaniel, to find out all about that adorable baby boy Heath was so happy to welcome into the world!

The Langley Legacy Series.....

FINN'S FORTUNE, by Kathleen Ball
PATRICK'S PROPOSAL, by Hildie McQueen
DONOVAN'S DECEIT, by Kathy Shaw
AIDAN'S ARRANGEMENT, by Peggy McKenzie
HEATH'S HOMECOMING, by Merry Farmer
COLLIN'S CHALLENGE, by Sylvia McDaniel

Be sure to sign up for my newsletter so that you can be alerted when all of these exciting books are released!

Click here for a complete list of other works by Merry Farmer.

ABOUT THE AUTHOR

I hope you have enjoyed *Heath's Homecoming*. If you'd like to be the first to learn about when new books in the series come out and more, please sign up for my newsletter here: http://eepurl.com/cbaVMH And remember, Read it, Review it, Share it! For a complete list of works by Merry Farmer with links, please visit http://wp.me/P5ttjb-14F.

Merry Farmer is an award-winning novelist who lives in suburban Philadelphia with her cats, Torpedo, her grumpy old man, and Justine, her hyperactive new baby. She has been writing since she was ten years old and realized one day that she didn't have to wait for the teacher to assign a creative writing project to write something. It was the best day of her life. She then went on to earn not one but two degrees in History so that she would always have something to write about. Her books have reached the Top 100 at Amazon, iBooks, and Barnes & Noble, and have been named finalists in the prestigious RONE and Rom Com Reader's Crown awards.

ACKNOWLEDGMENTS

I owe a huge debt of gratitude to my awesome project buddies, Kathleen Ball, Hildie McQueen, Kathy Shaw, Peggy McKenzie, and Sylvia McDaniel. This is what happens when a bunch of goofy people get together and stay up too late! And double thanks to Julie Tague, for being a truly excellent editor and assistant!

[Click here for a complete list of other works by Merry Farmer.](#)

Printed in Great Britain
by Amazon